TALE

The

and
The Tower

GERARD RONAN

Illustrated by Derry Dillon

libraries.
fingal.ie

ISBN: 9781914348020

For Eleanor

ONE PHONE CALL was all it took to destroy Rufus Black's family. One solitary phone call in the early hours of a rainy spring morning. Worst of all, it was Rufus who made it.

'9-1-1, what is your emergency?'

'It's Mom. I don't know what to do.'

'That's okay, honey. Just take a deep breath and tell me what's wrong.'

'She's bleeding. It's coming from her head.'

'Okay. Where's mommy right now?'

'On the kitchen floor.'

'Is she breathing?'

'I don't know. Dad pushed her, I think, there's blood on the worktop and on the floor. I think she hit her head.'

'And where's daddy at?'

'In the TV room, he's drunk.'

'Is that why you're whispering, because Daddy might hear you?'

'Yes.'

'How old are you honey?'

'Eleven.'

'Okay. Let me get someone right over to you. Where exactly are you at right now.'

'In the kitchen with Mom, please hurry. There's blood coming from her head.'

'It's okay, honey, I got that. Are you the only one there besides mommy and daddy?'

'There's the twins.'

'Are they with you right now?'

'No. They're asleep.'

'What age are the twins?'

'Three.'

'Is that boys or girls?'

'Girls. Annika and Chlöe.'

'And what's your name, honey?'

'Rufus.'

'Okay Rufus, this is what I want you to do. I

want you to stay on the phone with me. ⅃
you can do that?'

'I guess.'

'I want you to try and tell me what
happened.'

'I don't know. I heard them shouting and
then it stopped.'

'Just shouting? Nothing else?'

'No, just shouting. Is the ambulance
coming? There's lots of blood.'

'Yes, honey. Don't you fret. Help is on its
way. There's no one else in the house besides
Mommy, Daddy, and the twins, is that right?'

'No, no one.'

'And daddy. What's he doing right now?'

'I don't know. Sometimes when he's been
drinking he sleeps it off in the armchair.'

'Okay, Rufus. Help is almost there. Are the
doors all locked?'

'I think so?'

'Do Mommy and Daddy have cars in the

.l. It's a... I can't remember

, honey. Can you tell me the colour?'

'It's black... she's breathing... she moaned. I heard her moan. Wake up. Mom! Wake up.'

'Don't move her Rufus. It's important not to move her if she's hurt her head or neck. Now Rufus, listen to me, what colour is your front door?'

'Red. I can hear the sirens now, and I can see lights flashing, wait... (shouting in the background)... I didn't, I swear... I didn't... I just...'

'Rufus, is that your dad?'

'It was. He's gone. He's really mad. Why'd you have to send the police? I didn't ask...'

'Where's he gone, Rufus? He still in the house?'

'No. He went out back I think he's run off.'

4

'Okay, honey, we need to focus on Mommy right now. Is your phone the type you can walk around with?'

'Yes.'

'That's good. Now listen Rufus, I need you to take the phone with you and go open your front door. Are you able to do that?'

'Yes.'

'I'm gonna stay on the phone with you. My name is Tiana, by the way. You've done real good, honey. Your mom's gonna be so proud of you... Are you there yet?'

'I'm unlocking it now.'

'Okay, honey. When you open the door, I want you to give the phone to the officer. When he's happy the house is safe, he'll let the medics in.'

Before that night Rufus Black had thought his family would last forever. It didn't. His father disappeared and his mother took them away.

Far away. Away from their American friends and grandparents to a place they had only ever heard of in stories.

Rufus's mother could just as easily have decided to stay put. Had she done that he might have grown up to be an unremarkable American child who led an unremarkable American life.

But she hadn't. Instead, she had woken one morning in a hospital bed knowing with a fresh and solid certainty what had to be done. She knew because she no longer had anyone to turn to; because even the neighbours she liked had stopped calling round and would shrink from recognising her on the street. She knew, because someone other than her was caring for her children and, if she delayed any longer, they might yet be taken into care.

That morning, Susan Black checked herself out of hospital and went straight to the police. She had often warned Jonah what she would do if he ever hurt her. He would have known what was coming. Having done all that, and having collected Rufus and his twin sisters from the neighbour's house, she packed a suitcase and took a taxi to the bus station, from where she caught a bus to Chicago.

'We're going on a holiday,' was all she said by way of explanation. 'We could all do with a little adventure. It'll be a nice change.'

Ten days later the Blacks found themselves standing rain-soaked and anxious on the doorstep of a red-bricked terraced house in Dublin, Ireland. Back in Illinois, Susan had often spoken to her children of the heavy oak door that now confronted them; of how she had never forgotten the sound of its opening and closing, or the thud of the chunky brass knocker that her mother was forever polishing.

Thirteen years after she'd left, she still had a key. She was tempted to let herself in, but thought better of it. Drawing a slow, deep breath, she pressed the doorbell and waited.

'Yes?'

For a moment Lucy Harper seemed not to recognise her younger sister. Susan's face was a sorry mess and her hair was plastered to her head by rain.

'Susan?' said Lucy uncertainly.

Rufus could sense that his Aunt Lucy was stalling, and so too could the twins. He felt them squeeze his hands a little tighter.

'Long story,' said Susan meekly. 'Any chance of a bed until I get myself sorted?'

Lucy hesitated. Then, out of the corner of her eye, she caught the twitching of a neighbour's curtain.

'You'd best come in,' she said at length, 'and get out of those wet clothes.'

Susan hadn't been home since 1986 when she left for the U.S. on an athletics scholarship leaving her older sister to care for their widowed and ailing father. She had promised to do her fair share during the summer holidays, but she never came home. She got married and had a baby and 'Daddy' never forgave her. When he died he left the house to Lucy. Susan wasn't even mentioned in the will.

Lucy led Susan and the children to what had once been their bedroom and Susan instinctively threw her suitcase onto the upper bunk that as a child had always been hers. The twins top-and-tailed the bottom bunk, while Rufus spread a borrowed sleeping bag on the floor.

'This room's small,' whined Chlöe.

'Not small,' corrected Annika. 'TI-NY!'

'How long are we staying,' Rufus cut in.

'I don't know,' sighed Susan. 'I'm doing the best I can. You know that, right? Don't make this harder than it has to be.'

Later that evening, when she had put the children to bed, Susan told Lucy what had happened. It was obvious to Lucy that Susan had no intention of returning to Illinois. And that worried her, worried her greatly.

Susan and Lucy's mother had died giving birth to Susan when Lucy was just three years old. Lucy was the eldest, but it was Susan who had been their father's favourite. Jack Harper would drive for miles to watch Susan win a cross-country race, but he was always too busy to drive ten minutes up the road to watch Lucy play netball. 'Next time, Lucy, I promise,' he'd say. But next time never came.

Over the following days, as Susan made herself comfortable in a home that was no longer hers, eating food she hadn't paid for, Lucy's childhood resentment of her younger sister slowly began to resurface. She simply couldn't shake loose the suspicion that Susan intended to contest the will and claim a share of the house.

But she was wrong. Susan had no intention of staying. She had never felt adequate in that house. For her father, it had always been about winning. His love had always seemed dependant on it. And yet, she had never possessed the courage to deliberately lose a race and test him.

Four days later, after her stitches had come out and her facial bruises could be covered with make-up, Susan moved out. She took nothing from her old home, save for an old bike that had been gathering dust in the backyard shed. It had been her means of escape as a child. She would cycle for hours on it, seeking out places to explore. She would share it now with Rufus.

All the way from Dublin's Connolly Station to the coastal village of Donabate the children giggled and fidgeted excitedly, moving from seat to seat in the empty train to draw faces on the misted-up windows. But as their carriage began to roll across the viaduct that spanned the Broadmeadow Estuary, the giggling suddenly stopped.

A strange feeling swept over them. It could have been the surprise of seeing water on both sides of the train or the sudden realization that they were leaving the city behind. Whatever it was, by the time the train pulled into Donabate station, their approval of their new home had been all but guaranteed.

As he stepped down from the carriage, Rufus's eyes immediately lit upon the Victorian signal box. 'Look, Mom,' he said. 'It's like in the movie.'

'So it is,' said Susan. 'Like stepping back in time.'

Earlier that week the family had watched *The Railway Children* on TV. In this movie, an English family moved into a country cottage near a railway track, following their father's imprisonment on a charge of espionage. Towards the end of the movie, an old gentleman who befriends the children helps to prove their father's innocence and reunite the family.

On seeing that old signal box Rufus just *knew* that they would settle in Donabate; just as he knew that his father would someday return. He knew, not just because of the movie, but because he could taste salt in the air; because his father's name was Jonah; and because his mother had a tiny blue whale tattooed on her right ankle.

To Rufus, these things were like signposts on a road. They wouldn't be there if they led nowhere, would they? Some things were simply meant to be.

Their new apartment was situated on the top floor of a split-level house in a small estate to the west of the railway tracks. It had only one bedroom and Susan had furnished it with two bunk beds. The twins took the bottom bunks and Rufus and his mom took the tops.

The bedroom was tiny; as cramped as the room they had shared at Aunt Lucy's. 'It's all I can afford at the moment,' said Susan. 'We'll find better when we get settled.'

No neighbours came to introduce themselves or help them move in. But they didn't mind. They hadn't much stuff, and Susan didn't really want to be answering questions just yet. She had enough on her plate with school and childcare to be organised and a part-time job to be found.

Over the weeks that followed, as his mother searched for work and settled the twins into a local Montessori, Rufus was more or less trusted to look after himself. Borrowing his mother's bike, when she wasn't using it to cycle to interviews, he began to explore the wild green places of the Portrane peninsula, where everything seemed magical and unfamiliar.

He found secret ponds where all manner of

birds would gather and fields of wildflowers where colonies of frogs would hide. He even found a spot where he could spy on the farmers in the local park as they went about their work. Within a week there was scarcely an inch of the peninsula he hadn't explored, and even in those he had already discovered there was always something new to see.

His greatest joy came from his encounters with animals. In Newbridge Demesne he found squirrels and rabbits, and down at the beach the dunes were teeming with hares. Oystercatchers with long orange bills could be seen most days on the beaches and hardly a day passed that he didn't spot a buzzard or a kestrel out hunting for prey.

But special and all as they were, such encounters paled in comparison to the day he saw the kingfisher dart from a small stream near the Island Gold Club, or the pair of baby otters he came across one day in the

Broadmeadow River, or the day the horses came to the gate of a local field and allowed him to rub their heads and stroke their ears. He'd never had days like that in Normal.

His most extra-special encounter, however, came one balmy Saturday morning when the sea was like a sheet of blue-grey glass. As he explored the rocks that jutted into the tide north of Balcarrick Beach, a curious seal pup suddenly popped its head out of the shallows just feet from where he was standing.

'What have we got here then?' said Rufus softly, trying not to startle him.

The pup stared at Rufus, and Rufus stared back. Its eyes looked unnervingly human, especially when it looked sideways at him, revealing the white crescents in the corners of its eyes. The pup dived, resurfacing further out to sea, then looked back as if pleading with Rufus to come into the water and play. And he probably would have too, had he known how to

swim.

Instinctively, Rufus thought of running home to tell Jonah about the pup. But then it dawned on him that he could no longer tell Jonah anything. He didn't have a phone. He didn't even know Jonah's number.

Rufus missed his father. But simply admitting that made him feel disloyal towards his mother. He hated being pig-in-the-middle. His heart swelled in his chest, but he refused to cry.

For three days straight Rufus sat in that same place, waiting for his new friend to appear, speaking softly to him whenever he came close enough to hear him. If the seal wasn't there when Rufus arrived, Rufus would toss pebbles into the sea and, sooner or later, the pup would come to investigate, sniffing the air as if trying to catch his scent. Rufus decided to call him 'Sniffer'.

Each day Rufus would notice something new

about Sniffer: how he loved to do barrel rolls; how he appeared to have five webbed fingers for flippers; and how he could spend much longer under water than Rufus could hold his breath. He even fancied that Sniffer was starting to recognise him.

Not once, however, in all of his observations, did Rufus ever notice that, from a grassy bank above the rocks, he too was being watched, and just as intensely as he was watching Sniffer.

'Shush,' she whispered, placing a cool palm to his cheek. 'Go back to sleep. Mom's fine. We're all fine. It's just a dream.'

Back in Normal, they had lived so near to the Amtrak that Rufus had become deaf to the sound of passing trains. But here in Donabate, the sound served only to trigger nightmares about an argument that had started with some cross words about Jonah's laziness and ended with his mother lying in a pool of blood.

Rufus hadn't meant to call the police, just an ambulance, but the operator had sent both and the flashing blue lights had sent his father scurrying into the night without a word of farewell.

His mother had told him hundreds of times that he had done nothing to feel guilty about. But Rufus could never shake the feeling that, if only he had gotten a neighbour to drive his mother to the hospital instead of ringing 911, the family might still be together. If only he had gone downstairs and pretended to want a glass of milk the argument might have stopped. But he hadn't. And now it was too late.

His parents had been arguing for months. His father would always be sorry afterwards, of course, but Rufus knew that all the 'sorrys' in the world wouldn't amount to a hill of beans the next time Jonah went through a phase of not sleeping and turned to drink.

Sorry, to Rufus, was an empty word. Sorry was something you did, not something you said. Love wasn't meant to hurt; least not like that.

Susan would curse herself on these nightmare nights for having allowed her twisted relationship with Jonah Black to get so bad and for having continued to provoke him. It ought to have been her that suffered nightmares, not Rufus. She had never imagined, when decided to leave Normal, that she would ever end up feeling this guilty, or this lonely.

'Come on Rufus. Get a move on.'

Rufus woke to find Susan shaking him by the shoulder for the second time that morning. 'It's a school day, in case you've forgotten.'

He had. Ever since they moved to Ireland Rufus had struggled to remember what day it was. Back home he would map out his week by his favourite TV shows, none of which were available here. Dragging himself from his bed, he slid into his clothes and slouched to the breakfast table. Fifteen minutes later he was gone again, staring blankly at the back of the cornflakes box.

'For heaven's sake Rufus, shift yourself!'

'I hate school. I wish I didn't have to go.'

'Be careful what you wish for Kiddo! There are millions of poor children in the world who would gladly swap places with you. Get up and get a move on.'

On days like this Susan couldn't help remembering that Jonah, too, had been allergic to mornings. Only she didn't want to remember any of that. She wanted to forget, and she wanted her children to forget. She had even gone so far as to delete Jonah's number from her contact list, in case the kids might find it.

But Rufus didn't want to forget. He missed

his friends; missed baseball; missed peanut butter and jelly sandwiches; missed pancake and bacon breakfasts; missed the soothing afternoon thrum of cicadas outside his old bedroom. He even missed Jonah's corny jokes. If only he hadn't...

'RUFUS!'

Rufus jumped. Susan was not what you might call softly spoken. She was running late and racing to get the twins to Montessori, Rufus to school, and herself to the medical centre in Swords where she had found work taking the morning shifts as a doctor's receptionist.

Rufus went to take another spoonful of cornflakes.

'RUFUS!' Susan barked again. 'We haven't time. Leave that and get the twins into the car. I'll drop you off along the way.'

'KLOW-WEE!' Rufus bellowed in imitation of his mother's Dublin accent. 'ANN-IK-EH!'

His mother glared at him, daring him to repeat the mockery. Sometimes he was so like his father it hurt.

'C'mon Chlöe,' Rufus whined through the bathroom door. 'We're gonna be late.'

'Not my fault. You wouldn't get up.'

'Well, I'm ready now. And Mom's in a mood.'

In the bedroom, the word 'mood' sent Annika racing to present herself as ready and waiting. If Mom was going to 'blow', it would be Chlöe's fault, not hers. The twins rarely shared anything, least of all blame.

By the time Susan arrived at the car, the girls were silent, seated and belted, bookending the back seat like two curly-headed angels. Rufus had even found time, Susan noted, to tie Annika's shoelaces. Annika had yet to master a bow and Chlöe always refused to help. As for Rufus, he was sitting in the front passenger seat staring absently into space.

Susan took a moment to compose herself. Checking her hair in the rear-view mirror she started the engine, then paused. Something wasn't right. She could sense it.

'Rufus! Where's your school bag? For God's sake! You, of all people, know I can't afford to lose this job.'

Darwin Co-educational was the only private school for miles around. It was supposed to have been situated in a neighbouring village, but planning delays had forced the patrons to find a temporary home and so they had rented a four-bedroom family house in Donabate that had a garden large enough to accommodate several portacabins.

Sending Rufus to a temporary school was not ideal, but the village national school was full and Susan didn't want Rufus going straight into secondary school. The change would be too great to handle all at once. Better, all round, to have had some experience of Irish primary education and then start secondary school with the friends he'd made in primary. It seemed like a good idea at the time, though she had nurtured doubts about how he might fit in, he being already quite tall for his age.

'Darco' – as the school had quickly become known – had been established by the Irish Darwinian Trust, an organisation dedicated to fostering a love of science and critical thinking in children. The school was very much an experiment, and still finding its feet. Portacabins served as temporary classrooms and an enthusiastic staff somehow made it work. It was, after all, only meant to be for a year or two.

In line with the Darwinian theme, all of the classrooms were named after the wildlife of the Galapagos Islands, where Charles Darwin had framed his theory of evolution. Junior infants started in the Finch Cabin and progressed each year through birds and animals of increasing size. Rufus's class had the last cabin, the Giant Tortoise, from which students would graduate to secondary school.

From the very start, however, Rufus kept to himself, walking to and from school alone and making little attempt to find friends. A month after his enrolment he was still the 'new boy'; the tall unfriendly kid who insisted on spelling English words the American way.

Rufus was well aware of the impression he was creating. He could see it in people's reactions and hear it in the sniggers of Daisy Godwin and her little clique whenever he spoke in class. It made him feel dreadfully self-conscious and miserable. He longed to be back in his old school with his old friends. He didn't *want* to 'fit in'. He didn't *want* to 'adapt'. What he wanted, was to go home.

Another child might have reached out and found someone to talk to, but the very act of talking was filled with danger. A simple 'where are you from?' could lead to questions beginning with 'why?' and Rufus didn't want to go there right now. It was all too raw.

Recognising that he was struggling to 'fit in', his teachers were patient with Rufus; so much so that, when Rufus strolled sullenly into class that morning to find the vice-principal addressing the room, he was simply waved to his desk without comment.

'Miss Shalloo,' explained Mr Thomas as Rufus crept to his desk, 'has the flu, so I will be taking her class this morning. I thought we might begin with science. Does anyone know what we call the observation of stars?'

The class answered with a collective groan. Mr Thomas's classes might have been interesting had he occasionally brought a telescope or a video to show the pupils, but the most he ever did was draw diagrams. That morning, however, quite oddly and unexpectedly, someone managed to divert his attention.

'Astrology, sir.'

Everyone stared at the tiny boy in the front row desk. Nipper McVicar wasn't given to hand-raising in class, so this simply *had* to be a prank. Mr Thomas stared long and hard at him, searching for the slightest hint of insincerity.

'Not astrology, Craig,' he said at length, addressing Nipper by his proper name, 'but astronomy; a respected science. Astrology, dear boy, is mere superstition. Would anyone care to define superstition for us?'

A hand shot up at the back. Nothing new in that. But Miss Shalloo rarely invited Monika Pozniak to answer as it did little for a teacher's authority to be constantly corrected by a pupil. Monika, you see, was bright. Very bright. But Mr Thomas did not know that. He knew only that she was enthusiastic and that her eyes reminded him of a Siberian Husky. He motioned to her to answer.

'Superstition,' said Monika, 'means believing in things that are not true.'

Eyes bulged. Jaws dropped. First Nipper was volunteering answers and now Clever Clogs was being allowed to show off! Had the world been turned upside down or what?

'Not quite,' said Mr Thomas, unsettled by the stares of astonishment. 'It means placing your trust in something that is based on neither reason nor knowledge. For example, strange as it might seem, there are still people who believe that they can predict the future by observing the stars. Now…'

'Like psychics?' Daisy Godwin interrupted; her tiny voice almost lost in the inattentive din.

'Psychics?' said Mr Thomas, straining to locate the faceless voice and allowing himself to be further diverted from his chosen topic.

'Well, no. But rather than me explaining, why don't we try a little experiment, eh? A bit of critical thinking might be just the thing to wake us up on this dull and dreary morning.'

The class groaned, but Mr Thomas took no notice. From the pocket of his brown corduroy jacket, he pulled a two-euro coin.

'Right then,' he declared mysteriously, 'let's see if we have among us a potential master of the black arts, shall we? Stand up, please... QUIETLY!'

There were four tables in the portacabin and four children at each table. Each table was of a different colour: red, green, yellow, and blue.

'When I flip this coin,' said Mr Thomas, 'I want the red and blue tables to concentrate on trying to make the coin come down harps, and the yellow and green tables on making it come down heads. I said concentrate, Daisy, not suffocate. No need to hold your breath!'

Mr Thomas spun the coin in the air and

caught it on the top of his left hand, covering it with his right.

'Harps,' he declared, showing the harp side of the coin to the children. 'Those who were concentrating on harps remain standing. The rest of you can sit down.'

Noisily, the losers sat down. The class continued to be divided in two for every toss of the coin until there were just two pupils left standing: Rufus Black and Nipper McVicar – the tallest and smallest boys in the class respectively.

Glances and nudges were slyly exchanged, but not a whisper was heard. Nipper was told to concentrate on harps and Rufus on heads. Rufus closed his eyes and concentrated. Nipper merely cracked his knuckles.

Up into the air the coin went, spinning and spinning, as if time itself had slowed down. At the top of the toss it seemed to pause for a moment, then began to fall. As it passed his nose, Mr Thomas caught it in his right hand and slapped it theatrically onto the back of his left. Slowly and deliberately, he revealed the coin.

'Heads!'

'YES!' triumphed Rufus, oblivious to the raised eyebrows.

'Now then,' said Mr Thomas signalling to Rufus and Nipper to sit down, 'you have to admit that the likelihood of anyone correctly calling the flip of a coin that many times is pretty low. So, does that mean Rufus *made* it happen?'

The class laughed. A raucous, mocking laugh. Rufus went beetroot.

'ENOUGH!' Mr Thomas scolded. 'What I wanted you to learn is that sometimes, no matter how great the odds, a coincidence is simply a coincidence. Rufus here could have been thinking about his lunch for all the difference it would have made.'

Another ripple of mean-spirited giggles.

Mr Thomas rolled his eyes. He was beginning to regret having drawn attention to the flush-faced American boy whose discomfort reminded him of his younger self.

'Look,' he said. 'There was always going to be someone who'd been right every time. But did that mean that he made it happen or knew it would happen? Of course not! The same applies to horoscopes and psychics. If you say something vague about the future to enough people, eventually there will be someone for whom a series of predictions will ring true. Does everyone understand?'

Everyone nodded.

Everyone but Rufus Black.

Rufus knew differently. He didn't know how, and he didn't know why. It was just a feeling. A very strong feeling. Everything happens for a reason. That's what Jonah always said.

Rufus had always felt different, without ever being able to explain why. But following Mr Thomas's experiment, he no longer suspected that he was different: he *knew* that he was.

Two days later, the class repeated the exercise as a fair means of selecting who would be on clean-up duty, and once again Rufus was the last child standing. The only person *not* surprised at that, was Rufus Black himself.

And that was how his troubles began. The confidence with which he appeared to have been expecting the result triggered a lot of nudging and head-scratching. Daisy Godwin even began to see something sinister in his name.

'Rufus Black,' she'd remark to any who would listen. 'What sort of name is that? Creepy is what I call it. Don't you? He totally creeps me out.'

Rufus rarely discussed his nightmares with

his mother because to do so always led to questions in which he'd be asked to favour one parent over the other. But Jonah was still his dad, and, no more than anyone else, Jonah wasn't all bad.

The night that Rufus had phoned for the ambulance, a train was sounding its horn at a nearby level crossing. It was a small sound in the awful scheme of things, but it had stuck in his memory. And so, whenever the Belfast train raced noisily through Donabate, it inevitably brought back memories that Rufus would rather forget.

'Least I didn't cry,' he murmured absently as he took a carton of milk from the fridge.

'What was that?' said Susan, as she separated the whites for the weekend wash.

'Do you think Dad blames me for the cops?' asked Rufus. 'Is that why he hasn't called?'

Susan flinched. Rufus was finally talking about that night, but he wasn't taking sides.

She had always assumed that, when the time came, he would take hers. She, after all, was the one who ended up in hospital.

'I doubt the lazy drunk has given us a second thought,' she snapped back.

'That's not fair,' Rufus retorted. 'He wasn't always drunk, and he doesn't have to be like that forever, does he?'

'No, but...'

'And I only called an ambulance. If I...'

'Oh Rufus,' his mother cut in, softening her tone. 'He was always going to run. He was just waiting for an excuse.'

'But if I...'

'No buts,' said Susan. 'It had nothing to do with you. End of story.'

Only it wasn't.

When Jonah came back, thought Rufus, he would explain to him how he hadn't actually *called* the police, and then everything would return to normal. Because alcoholism was an illness, wasn't it? And nobody ever wants to stay sick, do they? And no matter what he'd done while drinking, Jonah had always been sorry afterwards. That meant that there was some goodness in him, didn't it? And a good father would not stay away forever.

As Susan ran a bath for the twins, Rufus slipped out of the apartment. He needed some time to himself.

'Going for a cycle,' he called as he pulled the door behind him.

Opposite the beach hotel, just a few metres from the water's edge, there stood a Martello Tower – a 19th century cannon emplacement designed by the occupying British forces to defend the Irish coast against Napoleon's navy. They'd learnt about it in school. Mrs Stern was a firm believer in children knowing something of the history of the locality in which they lived.

The cannons had been removed centuries ago, and the tower had long since been abandoned. But still, Rufus couldn't help imagining himself as one of those soldiers, taking turns at being a lookout, scanning the horizon for the masts of a French warship, watching for an enemy that never came.

He wondered how the soldiers filled the hours when they were not on watch or doing target practice on a cannon that would never be fired in battle. He imagined a lot of card games got played and a lot of stories got told. He wondered what kind of stories soldiers told each other. Battle stories, probably, or ghost stories at night. It wasn't as if they had TV back then.

Propping his bike against the tower wall, Rufus wandered down to the water and, while exploring the rock pools, happened upon a stick in a slimy knot of seaweed. It was the length of his forearm, the width of his index finger, and made of hard, blackened wood. It looked so much like a wand that Rufus soon abandoned the hunt for crabs to zap some imaginary dragons.

When he wasn't losing himself in a book, Rufus often invented stories; stories in which a tower became a castle, a beach became an island of buried treasure and the sea became an ocean of awe-inspiring monsters. And so there he was, dossing about on the rocks and waving his 'magic wand' when, all of a sudden, he felt a shiver run down his spine.

Instinctively, he turned.

A shadowy figure was staring in his direction. For a brief moment Rufus hoped it might be Jonah, but the figure was too short. So, who then? A thief?

He rushed back to his bike to find an old gentleman sitting next to it, on a large rock that lay close to the tower. The man had a polished black walking stick adorned with a

silver handle in the form of a human skull. The hand that held it was covered in a papery skin that looked so fragile that Rufus imagined the bones it covered might at any moment break through it.

Dressed in a black suit and a soft grey hat, the man wore a pair of circular dark glasses and sported a tightly clipped grey moustache. He looked vaguely familiar, and Rufus was certain he had seen him before, or at least someone a lot like him. Alas, try as he might, he couldn't place him.

'Wigs on the green,' the old gentleman sang in a thick Dublin drawl, 'big earwigs on the green.'

A patient from the nearby psychiatric hospital, Rufus thought briefly, then dismissed the idea. His clothes were too clean, his shoes too brightly polished.

'Big earwigs on the green,' the old gentleman sang on. 'Largest ever seen. Suffoclose!

Shikespower! Suedodanto! Anonymoses!'

Rufus spent a moment listening to him, spellbound by the rhythm and strangeness of his words. Then, all of a sudden, the old man stopped singing.

'Ah!' he hailed, as if the intrusion wasn't just welcomed, but expected, 'the sergeant-major with his swagger stick!'

'What was that you were singing?' asked Rufus, striving to appear casual. He knew he wasn't supposed to talk to strangers, but the old gentleman just seemed so frail and, well, respectable.

'Oh, just a little ditty to amuse me while I wait,' the old gentleman answered.

'Wait for what?' asked Rufus boldly.

'Why for you!' the old gentleman laughed. 'What is the first step; why is the last. Every story begins with an ending. Isn't that right? Nature lover, are you?'

'Some.'

'Used to love rock pools meself when I was your age; could spend hours exploring them. I'll bet you like animals better than people too. You have that look about you. You have a name son?'

'Black, sir,' said Rufus. 'Rufus Black.'

'Black you say, and with a big white head, like a resting pint of plain. Tell me, Master Black, what class of an accent is that?'

'American, sir. Normal, Illinois.'

'Normal, you say,' laughed the old man. 'How very ironic! You get my drift?'

'No sir, I don't,' said Rufus.

'Ah!' the old gentleman sighed. 'Then perhaps you're not the boy.'

'What boy?'

'The young creator, the apprentice extraordinary of the black and sinister arts.'

'You know?' gasped Rufus, suddenly aware that the conversation had become more than a casual exchange of pleasantries.

'Know!' exclaimed the old gentleman brightly. 'Why I'd hardly mention it if I didn't know. You'd best sit down, son, before your jaw falls off its hinges.'

Rufus kept his distance, a hand clasped in a protective fist about the fork of his bike.

'Sit,' the old gentleman commanded, beckoning him closer. 'I'm not the Devil.'

Nervously, Rufus sat, curious as to how the old gentleman could have heard about Mr Thomas's experiment in 'the black arts.'

'A long time ago,' the old gentleman said wistfully, 'I had a gift like yours and lost it. But I could help you to develop yours... if you're interested.'

'What gift?' said Rufus, forgetting again all he had ever been taught about talking to strangers.

'All in good time,' said the old gentleman, putting a vertical finger to his lips in a silent shush. 'But first, a test. Close your eyes and listen carefully. I'll tell you when to stop.'

Nervously, Rufus closed his eyes. To begin with, he didn't hear a thing but, ever so slowly, he began to hear it all: the plash of the incoming tide; the frop and snap of the hotel flags; the growl of a jet taking off from the airport; the convivial chatter from the hotel patio; the yap of a dog that had slipped his leash on the beach and the distant drone of a motorboat leaving the Malahide Estuary. He could even hear the occasional thwack of a golf ball from the golf course above the dunes.

In the space of just a few seconds, his hearing appeared to have become super sensitive. He wondered if that was what it was like to be blind. Afraid he might be about to lose his sight he opened his eyes. The old man was smiling.

'Impatient little scallywag, aren't you? Did I tell you to open your eyes? Close them now and tell me how many different kinds of birds you can hear.'

Rufus counted. A herring gull was yodelling out at sea; sparrows were twittering about the hotel patio, and there was what sounded like the chatter of a magpie from somewhere behind him. Finally, from its perch on the rocks, a solitary raven cawed.

'Four,' declared Rufus.

'Marvellous!' exclaimed the old man, patting Rufus on the knee. 'How many before?'

'None?' muttered Rufus, disturbed by the feel of an icy hand patting his knee.

'Excellent!' the old man laughed. 'Now, open your eyes and look out to sea.'

At first, Rufus saw only water. So he began to look around him, noticing things he'd never noticed before, like the black pimple on the summit of Lambay Island, the purplish outline of the Wicklow Mountains, and the hunch-backed shape of the Great Sugarloaf. Then, ever so slowly, he began to notice the water itself: the waves; the foam; and finally, the gulls, far out to sea, tiny as pinpricks in a blindfold.

It was the same as with his hearing: one minute he was seeing things with normal eyes and the next with a mysterious intensity. Had he really been born with super senses? How come he'd never noticed them before? How did the old man know?

'What colour is it?' asked the old man suddenly.

'What colour is what?' said Rufus, his attention snagged by an oystercatcher.

'The sea,' said the old gentleman, 'the scrotumtightening sea!'

There was something about the old gentleman that wasn't quite right; something eccentric in the way he spoke. Rufus didn't know what to make of it, but he liked that he wasn't like everyone else. It felt like they had something in common.

Rufus looked again. 'Lots of colours,' he said. 'All mixed up. Grey, green, black, white, silver, blue.'

'Anything else?'

'Cold... It looks cold.'

'Excellent! And what colour was it before?'

'Blue, I guess?'

'And suddenly you know differently. You know now that looking is not the same as seeing; that hearing is not the same as listening; that a colour is never just a colour, but a mood, a moment, a concoction. You are a gifted child, Master Black. Rejoice in your difference. Be proud of it.'

'Does that mean...'

'All in good time son,' the old gentleman cut in, 'All in good time. What you have is potential. What you make of it depends on how it fares when it is tested. Prove me right, and I'll share a secret with you that will change your life forever.'

'Tested!' groaned Rufus disappointedly.

'Nothing worthwhile comes easily,' the old man laughed, 'and this can only ever be between us. Understand? You can never tell another living soul. Not ever.'

Rufus nodded uneasily.

The old gentleman leaned on his cane and levered himself to his feet, his posture so stooped that he actually seemed smaller standing up. 'Well then,' he wheezed, 'go find a pretty girl, imprison her in a tower, and set her free.'

Rufus stared at the old gentleman, half-expecting him to laugh. He didn't. His eyes could have been laughing for all Rufus knew but, behind those dark glasses, it was impossible to tell if he even *had* eyes.

'Chew on it awhile,' said the old gentleman. 'No questions, no help. Now, show me that stick, and that stick pigstickularly.'

The old gentleman weighed the black stick

in his hand; then handed it back to Rufus.

'See if you can hit that rock over there.'

Rufus stared at the old gentleman. The stick was far too light to travel that far.

'Give it a go,' the old gentleman urged. 'If you miss, bring it to me and I'll show you a neat trick. All tricks and trumperies, that's me to a tea. Time for tea, I think. Nearly time for tea.'

The stick, as expected, fell well short of its target. Impatient to see the old gentleman do better, Rufus raced to retrieve it. When he turned around the old gentleman had gone.

'Back already?' his mother observed upon his return.

'Tide was in,' said Rufus, slumping into the armchair. He didn't like lying to his mother. His face nearly always gave him away. But if she knew he'd been speaking to a stranger his freedom to wander would be over.

'What's for lunch?' he asked, his tummy

rumbling.

'Lunch!' his mother exclaimed. 'You've only just had breakfast!'

The old gentleman's challenge consumed Rufus like a virus and helped muffle the sound of passing trains. Instead of waking each night, Rufus now tossed and turned, searching for a solution to a task he believed simply had to be a test of courage.

'Find a pretty girl, imprison her in a tower, and set her free,' the old man had said. The task seemed cruel, but then again, he'd been told to set the girl free, so it obviously wasn't with the intention of inflicting harm. The old man also hadn't said anything about the girl's age, so one of the twins, perhaps? Or Monika Pozniak?

Rufus liked Monika. She wasn't a giggly, girly girl. She was tender-hearted and pretty, in a tomboyish and very Polish sort of way.

Best of all, she thought well of herself and cared little for what others thought of her. Nobody made fun of *her* accent or *her* name. Nobody teased *her* for being tall.

Rufus was seven years older than the twins; Monika, six years older than her sister, Ania. Rufus's father had disappeared, and Monika's was an engineer who travelled so frequently that he was rarely at home. Had she been a boy, they might have been buddies. But she wasn't.

Monika had a pet tarantula called Ulryk. All Rufus would have to do to get her inside a tower, he imagined, would be to mention that he had seen an unusually large spider inside. But where could he find a suitable tower?

The following morning at school, shortly before line-up, Rufus found himself so absorbed in thought that he absent-mindedly walked into the back of Daisy Godwin.

'OUCH!' cried Daisy. 'That hurt.'

'Sorry,' mumbled Rufus meekly.

'Watch where you're going, Weirdo!'

'What?'

'You heard. *WEIRDO!*'

There was real venom in Daisy's tone and a stab of anger pierced his heart. He longed to lash out at her, but something held him back. Saying nothing, he simply drew himself up to his full height and stared furiously into her eyes.

'What's this,' laughed Daisy, 'the evil eye?'

By now Daisy was surrounded by a gaggle of girly-girls anxious to show solidarity with their exaggerated laughter. Another child might have buckled, but Rufus held his stare. What else could he do? To walk away now would be twice as embarrassing.

'*Weeeir-do!*' sang Daisy by way of a parting shot, stretching the word like the elastic of a slingshot.

'Yeah, *weeeir-do!*' chorused her friends,

drowning out the line-up bell.

Nobody thought any more of the incident until the following day when word reached the Daisy Chain that their ringleader had been rushed to hospital with suspected appendicitis. A fourth-class boy wondered aloud if Rufus had put a curse on her and the notion spread quickly throughout the school. By the time Rufus left for home that day he had been subjected to so many averted looks that it didn't take a genius to guess what the kids were thinking.

But Rufus didn't care. If they were going to label him a weirdo, he might as well be one. He'd much prefer to find his classmates nervous of him than laughing at him. It made him feel a little less invisible. He even began to wonder if Daisy's illness *had* been a coincidence. He'd been wondering a lot about such things of late.

The old gentleman was not like any person

that Rufus had ever met before. Indeed, from the very start, he could sense that there was something different, something special, about him. So, if he could sense that about the old gentleman, then why couldn't others be sensing the same about him? Maybe that *was* why Daisy got ill. Fear, after all, can do strange things to the body.

After school that day, Rufus cycled to Portrane. Turning into a patch of waste ground adjacent to the psychiatric hospital, he headed down a narrow track towards the round tower that dominated the headland.

It was a wild and gloomy afternoon. Small brown birds flew up occasionally from the long grass but, birds apart, he appeared to be alone. And yet, he just couldn't shake the feeling of being watched. Every now and again he'd hear something and turn, but there was never anyone there.

At a rusty farm gate, the path turned into a

narrow lane bordered by giant banks of bramble. He followed it until the track widened, then veered towards the abandoned psychiatric hospital: a red-bricked Victorian building with high chimneys that loomed so menacingly over him. In the dull afternoon light he found himself imagining faces in the cracked and flaking windows; feeling eyes upon him like a cold touch upon the spine.

At an old handball alley, a narrow path led away from the hospital and back towards the tower. It was thick with nettles that bit at his legs and got tangled in his wheels. Dropping his bike, he continued on foot, slashing at the thicket with a branch he found along the way, imagining himself hacking his way through an enchanted forest in search of a treasure his mind had yet to give a name to.

'Hello?' came a voice from behind the tower.

Rufus circled round to meet it. A young woman was sitting on a fold-up chair with a sketch pad in her hand.

'History buff, are you?' she asked, jokingly.

'Nah just exploring,' said Rufus.

'Excellent idea,' said the woman. 'Used to do a lot of that when I was young. Wanted to sketch the coat of arms for a local history project. It doesn't show up well in photographs. Bit of an oddity this tower. Not what it seems at all.'

'What do you mean,' asked Rufus.

'I mean it looks like an ancient round tower,' said the woman. 'But it isn't. It's actually a memorial to a local politician, George Evans. His wife, Sophia, built it, the first round tower to have been built in Ireland since the Norman invasion. And a very good copy it is too, but not an original. Never had any bells, you see, and you could never go to the top.'

Rufus looked up at the tower. It was over a hundred feet high. The entrance gate was ajar, but it was so high above the ground that he'd need a ladder to reach it.

'Funny thing is,' the woman went on, 'the tower is associated more with the bold Sophia these days, than her rather dull and earnest husband. An extraordinary woman, was Sophia, an early feminist and quite the practical joker by all accounts. Ah, but I can see from your expression that history is not your thing, perhaps I...'

'Do you know of any other towers around here?' Rufus cut in, totally disinterested in hearing anything more about Sophia Evans.

'Well there's an original round tower up in Swords,' the young woman said, 'and another over in Lusk. And of course, there's the tiny stump of one on Ireland's Eye.'

'I meant on the peninsula,' said Rufus. 'Around here, in Donabate or Portrane.'

'Just this and the two Martellos, I'm afraid,' said the woman, 'and of course that ugly water tower behind me. Stella's Castle in Portrane could possibly be called a tower, but it's really Norman tower house. Is that any help?'

'Not sure,' said Rufus.

'On a treasure hunt?' probed the woman. What's the clue, perhaps I can help.'

'It's not a treasure hunt,' said Rufus, turning on his heels before the woman could launch into another history lesson. Her answers weren't helping, and he didn't want to have to explain why.

Rufus had cycled past Stella's Tower on several occasions and knew it was not somewhere you could lock someone. But the two Martello Towers! *They* had roofs and doors. Someone lived in the one at Tower Bay so that was no good. That just left the one opposite the hotel, the one where he had met the old gentleman.

Balcarrick Beach was deserted when he got there, the weather being somewhat overcast, and there was nobody about the tower or on the hotel patio. Checking the tower door, he found it locked with a rusty chain and brand-new padlocks. An old chain, but new locks! That was odd in itself. It meant that someone had recently been inside. But locks were locks and, without the keys, there was no way to get inside. After another quick look to make sure the old gentleman wasn't hiding nearby, laughing heartily at his frustration, Rufus remounted his bike and cycled home.

The following day, during morning playtime, Rufus was sitting deep in thought, wondering if the old man's task wasn't actually a trial of courage, but a riddle of some sort. He never noticed Tomás and Francie approaching.

'Well if it isn't ol' Evil Eye,' said Francie, screwing up his face into a grotesque and mocking stare. 'Cast any more spells lately?'

'Get lost Francie,' said Rufus.

'Get lost Francie,' laughed Tomás, mocking

his American accent.

Why it should have happened then, he would never be able to explain, but Rufus snapped. All of a sudden he'd had enough of the mockery. He leapt at Tomás, fists flailing wildly, driving the pair of them onto the ground.

In the frenzied scrap neither managed to land more than a couple of close-range punches. The majority of the action was spent rolling in the wood chip, each trying to get on top of the other. To the casual observer, it would have looked more like a wrestling match than a fistfight.

Cries of 'Fight! Fight! Fight!' drew Mr Thomas running from his coffee break. Pulling the combatants apart by their collars, he checked them over for damage. Apart from Rufus's bloody nose, neither appeared to be any the worse for wear. The pair received playtime detention for the rest of the week.

Francie got off scot-free.

That evening, Susan sent Rufus to the Chinese for a take-away because she was too exhausted to cook. They ate directly from the cartons because she couldn't be bothered using plates that would have to be washed. And, having tried and failed to get the twins to bed, she delegated that task, too, to Rufus.

'Go on Rufus,' she pleaded drearily. 'Be a dote and read them their story. It's the least you could do after today.'

Rufus didn't argue. He knew better than to push his mother's buttons when she was that tired.

Annika liked fairy stories, but hated princesses. Chlöe loved princesses, but thought fairies stupid. There was no pleasing them both, so Rufus never gave them a choice. He simply pulled a book blindly from the wardrobe shelf and sat on the floor between their beds and read. That night, Fate had chosen Rapunzel.

'Once upon a time, in a faraway land,' he began, 'there lived a man and his wife.'

The twins weren't listening. They were giggling; enjoying a private joke at their brother's expense.

Rufus paused. 'Jeez guys, enough already! Do I have to take out the tickling fingers?'

'NOOO!' shrieked Chlöe joyfully, as Rufus reached for her ribs.

'ME TOO!' shrieked Annika, jumping onto Chlöe's bunk.

The twins loved being tickled and Rufus tickled them so hard that they laughed themselves to exhaustion. It was a game his father used to play with Rufus when Rufus was their age. He missed those days, missed them terribly.

It took a couple of minutes for the twins to settle down but, when Rufus picked up the book again, the exhausted pair cuddled snugly on either side of him on Chlöe's bunk.

'Once upon a time, in a faraway land,' he began again, 'there lived a man and his wife. They had a pretty little house and all they could ever need... except for one thing.'

By now Rufus was only half-attending to what he was reading himself because his eyes had landed on the tower in the illustration.

Could it really be that simple?

By the time Rufus had finished reading, the twins were ready for sleep. He carried Annika back to her bunk and tucked her in, then sat on the floor between their beds and waited for them to settle. When he was confident that they were drifting off, he leaned a hand on Annika's bunk to lever himself to his feet.

Annika turned.

'Rufus,' she whispered. 'When is Daddy coming home?'

'Up to him, I guess.'

'Does he know where we are?'

'Dunno. S'pect so. He has Mom's cell number and we still have the same e-mail.'

'So why hasn't he called?'

'Shoot! Annika, how should I know?'

Chlöe stirred. 'I miss him,' she whispered sleepily.

'I know,' sighed Rufus. 'Me too. Now go to sleep. It's late, and Mom's in a mood.'

The realisation that Jonah was not coming back took far longer to dawn on the twins than the realisation that they were never going home. But they never cried for the loss of either because in Rufus they had someone with whom they could safely remember.

Crying wouldn't bring Jonah back, or take them home. And crying would upset Mom. It was easier, all round, if they simply fell in line with her wishes, in the way families often do in order to keep the peace.

Leaving the door ajar to allow the twins

some light, Rufus climbed onto his bunk. 'Find a pretty girl,' he thought to himself. 'Imprison her in a tower. Then set her free.'

Three steps. A beginning, a middle, and an end. Didn't every story have those? Wasn't that what Miss Shalloo had taught them in school? Could it be that all the old gentleman had wanted him to do was write a story? A story with a happy ending?

Of course! He saw it now: it was a test of imagination, not a trial of courage. He felt strangely pleased with himself. Catching sight of his reflection in the wardrobe mirror, he became suddenly aware that he was changing. He didn't know how, and he didn't know why. He just knew that he was. He knew because he felt different, and, as he stared at his reflection, he quite fancied that he looked different too.

'Do my eyes deceive me, or is that Rufus

Black?'

A bony middle-aged woman with greying hair clipped up in a tiny bun and the faintest hint of a moustache on her upper lip, Judith Stern had the type of prim-and-proper personality that made you wonder if her surname really *was* an accident of marriage. She had been about to fill her second cup of coffee of the morning when she spotted Rufus strolling confidently into the wood-chipped back garden that currently served as the school playground.

'Half an hour early! And look at him... My God! He looks positively cheerful.'

From the old kitchen that functioned as the school staff room, arriving teachers gazed in amazement at the 'new' Rufus Black.

'Have you seen this?'

'What's happened to him? He's barely recognisable. I wonder if it has something to do with that scrap he got into yesterday?'

In choosing to hold himself apart, Rufus had wasted many opportunities to make friends. By the time he started edging closer to the games, hoping that a loose invitation might be casually thrown his way, it was too late. His presence had never been pointedly ignored: people had simply fallen into the habit of allowing it to pass unnoticed.

The Rufus who turned up at school that morning, however, no longer looked at the ground when walking or kept his hands in his pockets. With a spring in his step, he strolled about, head held proud as if though knew something important; something nobody else did. The change was immediately obvious to his teachers, but in the playground, too, his classmates began to notice.

'Goin' training tomorrow?' asked Nipper, referring to the under-age soccer team in which Susan had recently enrolled Rufus.

'I guess,' said Rufus uneasily. 'You?'

'Yeah. Got new boots for my birthday.'

Nipper McVicar was renowned as a serial prankster. You could never be sure that he was being serious. Earlier that month he had bought a white mouse, coloured its fur brown with a marker, let it loose in class, and then shouted, 'Look! A baby rat!'

In an instant the entire class was standing on their desks, the girls screaming as if they'd already been bitten. The panic spread so quickly, that the portacabin had to be evacuated. More recently, while on Friday clean-up duty, Nipper had smeared the whiteboard with Vaseline making it unusable on Monday morning.

Pranks like those, and his prodigious skill at soccer, had made Craig McVicar the coolest boy in school, and the boy most likely to be expelled. It was why he was always made to sit at the front of the class, where teachers could keep a close eye on him.

Rufus had already attended three of the soccer club's Thursday night training sessions and, on each occasion, Nipper had barely spoken to him. That made him suspicious of Nipper's motives.

'By the way,' said Nipper, 'it was brave of you to take on that pair yesterday. Everyone says so. You should try talking to people more.'

That brief moment of chumminess from Nipper, as much as his bravery in tackling Tomás, triggered a general change of attitude towards Rufus and, by lunchtime, he found himself the centre of unexpected attention. It was almost as if – one teacher was heard to remark – a spell had been cast upon him.

The riddle the old gentleman had set Rufus may not have been the ordeal that he had at first expected, but the solving of it had changed him. He could see that now. Every now and then he'd wonder how that had come about but, in truth, he didn't really care. He cared only that it would last.

Susan Harper first ran into Jonah Black on the graffiti-covered stairwell of Mother Murphy's Rock and Roll Emporium on West North Street, in Normal, Illinois. Texas-born Jonah was bounding up the stairs as Susan was hurrying down. They collided halfway.

'My fault, ma'am!' said Jonah, excusing himself in a broad Texas accent, but making no attempt to step out of her way. Their eyes met, and locked.

'Sorry!' said Susan, noting the slender physique and cropped blond hair. He looked more like a military conscript than a student, but he had a coarse charm about him.

'Jonah Black,' he said, offering his hand with a country-boy smile. 'Seen you running on campus.'

Jonah's family had come to Illinois from Fort Worth and, like Susan, he was an athlete, of sorts. For Jonah running was its own reward. He didn't need, or like, to race. He asked Susan out. She refused. He persisted.

'C'mon,' he said. 'What do you say? What harm in a cup of coffee? I was fixin' to have one anyways.'

A dozen flattering compliments later, Susan relented. By the end of the month, she was madly in love. One blissful year later she was married with a baby boy and a tiny blue whale tattooed on her ankle. By then she had lost her scholarship and Jonah had had to quit college and find a job to support them.

Their lives had been turned upside down, but they were as happy and smug as any pair of first-time parents. They even managed to get out for the odd run together on the Constitution Trail at weekends, pushing baby Rufus along in a special jogging stroller they'd picked up cheap at a yard sale.

Despite his parents' passion for the sport,

Rufus found running boring. Baseball, on the other hand, was exciting. Baseball was a man's game. Whenever they discussed baseball, Jonah and Rufus would argue and joke like best friends. No matter how bad things got at home they could always talk about baseball.

Back in Normal, Jonah had taken Rufus to play Little League Baseball every Saturday morning. And Rufus wasn't half bad. But nobody played baseball in Ireland and to stop him pining for his old friends, Susan had dragged Rufus down to the local soccer club and enrolled him in an underage team.

'More exercise and less moping. That's what you need. Might even help you to sleep better.'

'But Mom! Soccer's a girls' game.'

Back then soccer was considered a girls' game in the USA. And Rufus didn't even know the rules. Add to that his tendency to daydream in the middle of a game and you had a recipe for disaster.

The kids gave up on him almost immediately; the coach not long after. 'You can't get feathers from a frog,' he heard Scrawny Butler, the team coach, remark one night, after which Rufus gave up all pretence of trying. Had Susan not forced him out the door each Thursday evening, imploring him to give it time, he'd have given up long ago.

But everything had changed since he met the old gentleman. The curse of invisibility had been lifted and at Thursday night five-a-side people suddenly began to notice him.

'New trainers Rufus?' enquired Scrawny.

'No, sir,' said Rufus. 'Why?'

'Dunno,' said the coach. 'You just look, taller somehow.'

Now that his head wasn't permanently bowed, Rufus appeared more attentive. It took a little while for the boys to start passing the ball to him, but once they did he repaid their confidence in spades.

Now that he was standing tall, Rufus found that he could read the game more easily. Realising that he wasn't fast enough to go past people, he started playing the ball into the space behind the opposing team's defenders, giving Nipper a chance to get a head start on them as they turned.

The first time Rufus did this, Nipper was taken by surprise and was late to the ball. The next time Nipper was waiting, and scored.

'Fluke,' the blue bibs chorused.

But then Rufus did it again, and again. He never scored himself, but from the seven passes he threaded through the crowded defence, Nipper scored three times and the red bibs won.

'Keep this up Rufus,' shouted Scrawny, 'and you'll find yourself starting before long.'

Rufus beamed. He could scarcely believe what was happening to him. He wished Jonah could see him.

After training everyone seemed keen to include Rufus in the dressing-room banter. They teased him good-naturedly about his height and shortened his name to 'Roof'. He liked that. He'd never felt comfortable with his name, and neither had Jonah, who had always addressed him as 'Sport' or sometimes, as simply 'Kid'.

'Roof' wasn't perfect, but it suited Rufus just fine. It didn't sound like a dog's name and made him feel like he belonged. It was only a word. But it was a powerful word.

Rufus fairly bounded up the stairs when he got home that night, taking the steps two at a time and almost missing the final one to the landing. He burst into the apartment to find Annika tormenting Chlöe.

Earlier that day Susan had bought the twins packets of white chocolate buttons. Chlöe had gobbled hers immediately as usual, but Annika had saved hers for later and was now taunting her sister by eating them ever so slowly in front of her.

'Supposed to share.'

'Am not. *You* didn't.'

'MOM-MY!'

Normally Susan would have avoided scenes like this by insisting that the twins ate at the same time or not at all. But that afternoon she had caught sight of a woman in a shop window and had been halfway to a judgemental thought before realising that the bulging reflection was her own.

Rufus knew nothing of this. All he knew was that Chlöe was bawling like a hyena and that his mother was unusually silent. It wasn't like her not to intervene. Ignoring his squabbling sisters he raced, somewhat alarmedly, to the kitchen.

He found Susan standing in front of the washing machine holding an old tracksuit top that she had recently rescued from Lucy's attic. It no longer fit her, but it reminded her of how it felt to be young. She longed to be able to run again, to be even half the person she had been then. If only she could find the time!

Oblivious to his mother's sorrows, but relieved to find her okay, Rufus prattled excitedly. He told Susan about the wonderful night he'd had, and about his new nickname.

'Roof! Get it, Mom? Because I'm so tall. It was weird, Mom. Really weird!'

'That's nice, Rufus,' said Susan absently. 'I'm so pleased. See what happens when you make an effort. Now be a dear and put the twins to bed, will you?'

Saturday morning was cold and a heavy fog had settled on the waves. The old gentleman sitting in his usual spot, staring out to sea as if his eyes could somehow penetrate the mist. Sensing he was being watched, he stirred.

'That you?' he said without turning.

'It's a story,' shouted Rufus, racing to close the distance between them. 'The test was to write a story. I'm right, aren't I?'

For a moment the old gentleman seemed pleased. But then his eyes lit on Rufus's empty hands and he turned away again.

'Arrah why, says I, couldn't you manage it?' he groaned poetically.

'I couldn't think of one,' said Rufus weakly.

'Dream, do you?' said the old man.

'Everybody dreams!' replied Rufus distractedly. 'But I only remember mine if they're scary. And my name's Rufus, not *Boy*.'

'Ah yes, the young master. Well then, *Rue Fuss*, Mister 'anything for the quiet life', remember the dreams you have while you're awake. Find your stories there, where the tall stories grow proudest.'

'That's stupid,' Rufus protested.

'You think so? Then maybe you're just an ordinary boy after all. An ordained airy boy with a big nonobli head, and a blanko berbecked fischial ekksprezzion'

'And maybe you're mad!' Rufus retorted.

'MAD! Says he,' the old gentleman laughed. 'Better mad, says the old fool, than lazy.'

Stung by the rebuke, Rufus turned to pick up his bike.

'You'll be back,' said the old gentleman without turning. 'As sure as there's a pot on a pole. You'll be back.'

Rufus missed having a father figure to talk to. It was why he generally enjoyed chatting to the old gentleman, and why he now regretted the manner of their parting. In an effort to repair the relationship, he decided that he would prove to the old gentleman that he wasn't lazy; that he really was special.

But it wasn't easy. The more he tried to think of a story, the harder it became to imagine one. The more he tried to remember his dreams, the less he seemed to remember. He'd almost given up trying when, late that same evening, he had an idea. Leaping from the sofa, he went to his bunk and started to scribble:

Once upon a time there was a boy called Edward who discovered that chewing the leaves of a plant at the end of his garden, made him invisible. He liked the idea of being invisible. It made it easier to spy on people. But every time he chewed a magic leaf, he became invisible for longer and longer. Soon he could no longer control how long he would remain invisible for.

It wasn't easy being invisible. He had to be careful crossing the road and to make sure that people didn't bump into him. He also had to be totally naked, for only his body that became invisible, not his clothes.

While he was invisible, he began to hear

what people actually thought about him. It wasn't nice. He began to imagine ways in which he could use his invisibility to get even. But one day he chewed too many leaves and couldn't make himself visible again.

It was a rough start and Rufus didn't yet know how it was going to end. He understood now what the old gentleman had meant about every story beginning with an ending. The harder he tried, the more frustrated he became, until at length his mother began to notice.

'Rufus! It's almost eight. Would you mind reading the twins their story?'

'Aw, Mom!' moaned Rufus. 'I've loads to do.'

'You've been at it for hours. What could you possibly have left to do?'

'Alright, alright,' growled Rufus storming off. 'I'll read them their stupid story!'

'RUFUS!' his mother called after him, but

Rufus didn't look back.

While he was gone, Susan picked up her son's maths copybook and started to read. When he came back, she was waiting for him.

'What's this?' she said, holding his copybook.

'A story I'm writing,' mumbled Rufus.

'For school?'

'Not exactly.'

'Where's your homework? I want to check it.'

'We're supposed to do it ourselves.'

'Show it to me.'

Rufus refused to move.

'NOW!' his mother shouted angrily.

'You'll wake the twins,' said Rufus, sarcastically stoking his mother's temper.

'I don't care if I wake the bleedin' dead,' retorted Susan. 'I'm not having the principal calling me in to tell me you're falling behind. This school is costing me an arm and a leg as it is. Now show me your homework.'

'I haven't started it yet.'

'Then start it now. If you want to write stories, you can write them when you've finished. No TV until it's done. I mean it.'

Susan was worried. In her youth, she had always gone for a run or a cycle whenever she felt troubled or lonely. That was why she had allowed Rufus to take her bike so often. Retreating into the world of books or stories had been Jonah's way, not hers. She didn't think it was healthy, for adolescent boys could be cruel and bookworms might just as well be hanging a placard around their necks and asking to be bullied. Rufus had gotten into one fight already. Was there more he wasn't telling her?

Next morning, Rufus' head was swimming with ideas for his story. They came in dribs and drabs and always at unexpected moments. Each time he would be desperate to write them down before they were forgotten.

The latest came just as he was passing the front doors of the shopping mall. As he fumbled in his schoolbag for some paper, he failed to notice Francie and Tomás exit the supermarket.

'Wotcha doing?' sneered Francie, stuffing half a sausage roll into his mouth.

'Nothing,' said Rufus.

'Gis' a look,' laughed Tomás, grabbing Rufus in a chokehold while Tomás tore Rufus's maths copybook from his hands.

'Give it back,' shouted Rufus.

Francie held Rufus while Tomás scanned the pages. Rufus felt a lump rise in his throat.

'Invisible!' laughed Francie out loud, finally spotting the notes at the back. 'Magic leaves? You writin' a book or sum'in? Well?'

Rufus could feel the heat rising in his face, but before it could reach his eyes, the supermarket door slid open, and out sauntered Nipper McVicar, looking oddly dapper in a flat tweed cap.

'Give it back,' shouted Nipper quickly.

'Wot's it to you,' snarled Francie, doing a double-take at Nipper's cap.

'Just give it back,' said Nipper forcefully.

'You gonna make me?' snarled Francie.

'Not me,' said Nipper calmly. 'My dad. He's coming right behind me.'

Francie swapped an uncertain glance with Tomás. 'Leg it!' he laughed, racing towards the school, tearing pages from Rufus's maths copybook as he ran.

'Chickens!' shouted Nipper after them, though not so loud as to tempt them to stop.

'You okay, Roof?' asked Nipper kindly.

'Fine!' snapped Rufus, wishing the ground would open up and swallow him as he gathered up the torn pages.

'What's up, guys?' It was Monika Pozniak's turn to steal up on him.

'Rufus has had another run-in with the

Gruesome Twosome,' said Nipper matter-of-factly.

'Nice hat!' said Monika, with a little grin.

'Thanks,' said Nipper, blushing.

'Shame about the face!' she added mischievously.

Nipper thought about responding in kind but settled for cracking his knuckles.

'GROSS!' squirmed Monika. 'I really wish you wouldn't do that.'

'Do what?' said Nipper. 'This?'

He cracked his knuckles again.

A shiver ran down Monika's spine. She hated when people did that.

'Did they hurt you, Rufus?' asked Monika softly, peering intently into his swollen eyes, her hand resting gently on his shoulder.

'NO!' snapped Rufus, pulling away. 'It's not them. My dog died. He slipped his leash and got hit by a car.' Even as he spoke, Rufus felt the shame and the lameness of his excuse.

'I didn't know you had a dog,' said Monika, twirling a plait of her hair. 'That's so sad. I'd be devastated if anything happened to Ulryk.'

Ulryk was Monika's pet spider – a five-year-old redleg tarantula that she fed on crickets and the occasional pinkie mouse. But Ulryk was real. Rufus's dog was not. Or not exactly.

Back in Normal Rufus *had* owned a black Labrador called Jet, and Jet *had* died following a collision with a USPS truck on Franklin Avenue. But that was two years ago. He prayed the questions would stop there. He was feeling small enough as it was.

Luckily Nipper and Monika felt uneasy at the mention of the dead dog and feared to say anything that might tempt Rufus to tears. The intervention of the lollipop lady helped too. She had a little laugh at Nipper's flat cap and called him Farmer Brown. Nipper and Monika laughed, and Rufus carried the shame of his pathetic lie in silence.

Shortly after roll call that morning, Miss Shalloo decided to correct the children's maths homework.

'I want everyone's maths copy on my desk now. Molly, will you please collect them.'

The children piled their copybooks at the end of each table and Molly McCall collected them. Monika looked to Nipper, and they both looked to Rufus, who refused to meet their gaze.

'OK, who am I missing?' said Miss Shalloo.

Rufus half-raised his hand.

'And what's your excuse? And don't tell me the dog ate it.'

Out of the corner of his eye, Rufus caught sight of Monika shifting in her seat. He shot her a severe look. It stopped her, but only temporarily.

'Go on then,' said Miss Shalloo.

'I lost it,' Rufus mumbled.

'LOST IT!' exclaimed Miss Shalloo. 'Is that

the best you can do? Well then?'

Rufus stared silently at his feet, his eyes clouding at the prospect of yet another humiliation. Tomás gave a nervous snigger. That was the last straw for Monika. 'He didn't lose it, Miss, it was stolen.'

Rufus went beetroot. He shot another look at Monika, but it was too late.

'Stolen!' Miss Shalloo laughed. 'That's certainly a new one on me. Care to explain?'

'It's true Miss,' interjected Nipper, coming to Monika's aid. 'We were there. Francie and Tomás took it off him outside the supermarket.'

'They're lyin' Miss,' said Francie. 'We never touched his copybook.'

'You did too,' countered Monika. 'And you tore lots of pages out of it.'

Miss Shalloo turned her eyes to Rufus. 'Is this true?' she asked, her tone softening.

Rufus said nothing. He just stood there,

trembling. If the dead dog story didn't do for him, Francie and Tomás certainly would.

'Right then, you two, come with me. The rest of you open your maths book on page fifty-three. Do the first six questions, and if there's a peep out of anyone while I'm gone there'll be hell to pay.'

'You're dead, Yank,' snarled Francie as he passed Rufus's desk.

At lunch break Rufus was standing by himself, wallowing in self-pity, worrying about how the gruesome twosome would get even. He never noticed Monika approaching. Before he could pull it away, she had taken his hand and started to tie a woollen friendship band around his wrist.

'Welcome to the Half-Blood Club,' she said, looking into his eyes in that intense way of hers.

'The what?' said Rufus, feeling himself blush

but unable to look away.

'My father's Polish,' she said as she tightened the knot, 'and my mother is German. So my blood's half Polish and half German, like yours is half American and half Irish. We half-bloods have to stick together.'

Rufus wasn't listening. She'd lost him at *club*. He simply couldn't imagine any of the kids in that school wanting to be in a club with Spider-Girl.

'Who else is in this club?' he asked warily. 'It's not just me is it?'

'Can't tell you just yet,' said Monika, tapping her nose in a conspiratorial fashion.

'So, there *are* others?'

'There might be. Look, I'm sorry about your dog, Rufus, but if you want to start collecting tarantulas I know a shop where you can get some. They live for thirty years. That's twice as long as dogs!'

'Thanks, but no thanks. My mom can't even

stand the little ones that creep out of the plughole in the bath.'

That afternoon, as Monika and Nipper walked Rufus home from school, it suddenly struck Rufus that something else had changed since he met the old gentleman. For the first time since he arrived in Ireland, he had friends: real friends! And by the looks of things he was going to need them.

'Cock of the wark!' the old gentleman exclaimed. 'You have a story. Now write it.'

'But I have written it!' Rufus protested, handing him the new copybook he'd taken from the cupboard to write his story in.

'Written!' The old gentleman laughed. 'This is but a sketch. What a quhare soort of a young mahan you are! Drawing con tours instead of land escapes; lying in your lazybed and admiring the blight.'

Rufus was stunned. Teasing he could deal

with. But criticism! Someone telling him that his work wasn't good enough! Even his teachers sugared their criticism with praise. He turned to pick up his bike.

'Running away won't help,' said the old gentleman. 'But you know that already, don't you son?'

Rufus paused, wondering if the old man was referring to his family situation or to the situation in which he'd found himself at school.

'Come, sit down,' the old man insisted.

Rufus hesitated. The last thing he needed was a talking-to, but grown-ups only made you sit when they wanted to get serious.

'You like toffee?' the old gentleman asked.

'I guess?' answered Rufus.

'Don't you know?'

'Alright then. Yes, I like toffee.'

'Then have a chew, bought today, good as new.'

The old gentleman pushed a brown plastic

bag towards him, and Rufus took a toffee. Every now and again he would glance back at the old man, wondering when the lecture would start, but the old gentleman just sat there, staring out to sea.

It took a minute for Rufus to notice what the old gentleman was staring at – a black blob beyond the breaking waves that was there one minute and gone the next.

'Friend of yours?' asked the old man.

'It's Sniffer,' said Rufus.

'Given him a name already I see,' said the old man. 'I wonder what he calls you!'

'Nothing, I s'pose. He's just a seal.'

'*Just* a seal, says he! They were never *just* seals to my generation. Back in the day people believed they were humans cast under a spell. Selkies, they called them.'

'That's stupid,' said Rufus disdainfully.

The old man ignored him and rose to his feet. 'In the beginning, was the word,' he trumpeted loudly, waving his arms about as though preaching from a pulpit, 'and the word became flesh.'

Rufus didn't know where to look. Passers-by turned to stare and to laugh at the old man's antics. Beyond the rocks a seagull yodelled, interrupting the old gentleman's flow. He paused to allow the gull to finish, then resumed his seat.

'Give your characters a life, son,' he said in a lower voice, 'and they'll live forever. They might even share something of their immortality with you, like Mr Scrooge did with Mr Dickens. Put flesh on the bones, son. Fresh flesh on the bones. Take this character you've created – Edward, isn't it? Make him believable. What you have here is a skeleton. Put flesh on the bones, son. Fresh flesh on the bones.'

Unaccustomed to criticism, Rufus fought back.

'What makes you such an expert?' he protested. 'I mean if you're so good, why aren't you writing books instead of sitting here all day?'

'What I have or haven't done is none of your business,' the old gentleman barked defensively. 'But if this is how you receive well-intentioned advice, then perhaps I'm wasting my time: the poorest commonon-guardiant waste of time.'

'Yeah, maybe!' said Rufus sourly.

'Then at least it is mine to waste,' the old gentleman sighed. 'But waste your own and you'll become just another grey seal in the great grey ocean. Is that what you want? To be ordin-airy?'

Sullenly, Rufus got up to leave, but the old gentleman wasn't about to let him go without a fight. 'Who, what, where, when, why, and how,' he added, his voice softening. 'Sound familiar?'

Rufus hesitated, but didn't respond. Of course he recognised them. They were the tools you needed to tell a story. He'd been made to recite them at least once a month in English class back in Normal.

'Well then,' said the old gentleman, 'before you slink away to sulk in some dark corner, consider the possibility that you may have mislaid a couple. Take this chap, Edward. We never learn what he looks like, or how old he is; neither his livin' drames nor his sleepiest fares. How then are we to picture him? Don't take the poor craytur for grafted. Nurture him, Rufus, nurse him to maturity.'

'It's just a story,' grumbled Rufus, staring at his feet. 'And you're just a lonely old man.'

'And what does that make *you* then? How desperate must *you* be, to hang around with a soul as pathetic as you've just described? And in far more detail, I might add, than you described young Edward, the poor craytur.'

'I worked hard at that story!'

'Shite and onions!'

'Did too.'

'Really? Was that truly your best effort? Just look at your opening line. Once upon a time. What age are you son? Four? Five? When was the last time you read a story that opened like that?'

Rufus blushed. The old gentleman had a point. He *was* too old for fairy stories.

The old gentleman leant on his walking stick and levered himself painfully to his feet. He began to sing. 'Have you heard of one Humpty Dumpty, how he fell with a roll and a rumple...' He stopped abruptly and pointed. 'Look, over yonder,' he then said. 'On the rocks. What do you see?'

'A man,' Rufus mumbled. 'Fishing.'

'Fishing?' said the old man. 'With what? Fish attracted to the rod, are they?'

'Nah,' Rufus mumbled, 'to the bait.'

'Exactly!' the old gentleman exclaimed. 'It's the same with stories. You have to hook your readers first, *then* reel them in. Every word you write should have but one purpose – to manipulate the bate of the human heart. Words, Rufus, are the most powerful things in the universe.'

Rufus winced at the word 'powerful'.

'Listen,' the old man went on, 'which would make you want to keep reading: *Once upon a time there was a beautiful princess...* or... *it had been almost ten years since she'd set foot outside that room?*'

'The second?'

'Hit the pipe, dannyboy!' the old man exclaimed. 'Now take another toffee and conjure up a line for me. Make it bold and dramatic. Chew on it a while, mould it into shape.'

Rufus chewed, and chewed, but succeeded only in summoning a lot of unconnected images. To make matters worse, every now and again the old man would place a cold palm on his knee. It wasn't an aggressive touch – more a friendly pat – but it made Rufus uneasy. He had never felt a touch so cold. He longed to edge away but felt unable to, as though a spell had been put on him that would lift only when he solved the puzzle.

A while later, his attention diverted by a barking dog, Rufus had a flash of inspiration. 'Got it!' he trumpeted, astonished that the idea had come to him at the very moment he hadn't been trying.

'Go on, then,' said the old gentleman. 'Drop it on the ears.'

'In the space of seven days,' Rufus recited uncertainly, 'Edward went from being the child that no one noticed, to being the child that no one could see.'

'Three quarks for Muster Mark!' triumphed the old gentleman. 'There's hope for you yet!'

'But that was one line,' protested Rufus. 'Do I have to work that hard on every line?'

'Every lion and tiger, but if the story truly matters, son, you'll agonize over every snakey syllable. You'll take your time and you'll do it for yourself. You will understand why it has to be you, and why there is not another living soul that can do it for you.'

'No gods, no ghosts, no goblins!'

'Nice alliteration. One of yours is it?'

'Something my dad used to say.'

'Had a way with words, too, I see,' said the old gentleman. 'Perhaps there's more of him in you than you realise. Flawless diamonds are extraordinarily rare. Try to remember that when next you rush to judgement.'

Rufus hadn't liked being compared to his father, had even come to dread looking in mirrors in case he'd see something of Jonah's face in his own. But after an hour of television, that evening his anger cooled and he went to his bunk. Maybe, just maybe, he thought, if he took things slowly, and dealt with the story one small piece at a time?

Opening his copybook Rufus read the opening line of his story, then crossed it out. Sitting on his bed, he stared into space, trying one idea after another until, out of the corner of his eye, he spotted a woodlouse crawling from under the skirting board. The inspiration was instant.

It was the caterpillar that started it. The caterpillar that was there one minute and gone the next. Noticing how the leaf on which it sat was still being eaten, the boy began to wonder. Were his eyes deceiving him? What if he were to...

Rufus looked up at the clock. An hour had passed in the blink of an eye. What was happening to him? Every time he put pen to paper, he seemed to lose a whole chunk of his life, a precious chunk he could never get back.

Rufus was waiting in the queue for the bathroom when Nipper pulled him aside.

'Heard about Horse?' he said.

'What horse?' said Rufus.

'Not what, who! Horse Tourney. Tomás's dad. Got six months for assault. It was in all the papers.'

Rufus felt his stomach churn. He worried about what having a dad in prison would do to Tomás. To make matters worse, Francie had returned from suspension with a black eye. He'd only been suspended for two days but he'd been absent for four. Nobody had to ask how it happened.

Rufus never received the expected beating, but he could hardly turn his back without finding chewing gum in his hair or spilt milk in his bag. One day his coat even went missing and he had to walk home in the torrential rain without it. Nobody saw Tomás or Francie do any of this, but everyone knew who was responsible.

'What are you going to do?' asked Monika one day. 'You can't let them get away with it.'

'Nothing,' said Rufus shortly.

'You can't do nothing,' said Monika. 'They won't stop unless you do.'

'Telling wouldn't help,' he said. 'They'd just find other ways to get even and I've too much on my plate to be worrying about them.'

'Is it because of that story you're writing?'

'Kinda,' said Rufus. 'Can't seem to finish it.'

'Would you like some help?'

'No!'

'Only asking! Sometimes it's good to ask for help. I know you said your mom thinks it's a waste of time, but maybe your father could help.'

Rufus went pale.

'He can't. He's gone... I mean... I don't have a dad. He isn't dead or anything. Just ran out on us. That's why Mom brought us back to Ireland.'

'That's awful, Rufus. Do you miss him?'

'I guess. But look, no one knows about this. You have to promise not to tell.'

'Not even Nipper?'

'Especially not Nipper. Promise?'

'I promise, Rufus. I won't.'

Rufus felt lighter for having told Monika. But then he hadn't told her that Jonah had a drink problem or that he'd hit his mother. But he might have, had she pressed him, and that worried him. He'd already betrayed one parent.

In his heart, Rufus knew the old gentleman wouldn't be impressed with his lack of progress on *The Invisible Boy*. But he was stuck. He'd cycled to the beach hoping the old gentleman might suggest an ending to his story, but as he parked his bike his heart sank. The old gentleman was sitting against the wall of the tower, stabbing aggressively at the ground with his stick. He was having a cranky day.

Rufus thought of calling out to him, but suddenly realised he didn't know his name. He'd never asked, and it was too late to do so now. Hearing him approach, the old man turned. Rufus presented his copybook.

'What are you giving it to me for?' said the old gentleman irritably.

'I need help,' said Rufus. 'I did what you asked, but I still couldn't make the words read like they do in books. I couldn't even find a way to end it.'

'Thought it would be easy, did you?'

'No, sir. I thought you'd help, s'all.'

'Sit,' the old gentleman commanded as if

speaking to a pup. Up close the old gentleman's cheeks showed the tracks of what Rufus took to be tears. Was it the wind? Or had he been crying?

'Show me what you've written.'

Rufus handed him the copybook and the old gentleman took from the breast pocket of his coat three coloured pencils: one red, one green, and one blue.

Over and over the old man read, making a correction here and a suggestion there, sometimes even correcting his suggestions or refining corrections he'd already made, swopping one coloured pencil for another in some secret method he never explained. After a while, he let loose an exasperated tirade.

'Said! Said! Said! Where's the emotion in said. How did they say it, eh Rufus? Sighed? Groaned? Yelled? Cried? Whispered? Moaned? Just because you can hear them speaking doesn't ' mean anyone else can. Do you understand?'

Rufus nodded. He didn't particularly like the old gentleman's tone, but he'd asked for his help.

'And look at the length of these sentences,' the old gentleman went on. 'What were you thinking? What was the first power we explored?'

'Hearing?' answered Rufus, a lump forming in his throat.

'And have you? Well? Have you listened to these sentences? I mean really listened?'

'I've read them over and over. Lots of times.'

'I didn't ask if you'd *read* them.'

'Oh,' said Rufus, belatedly wise. 'You mean I'm supposed to listen to them? To read them out loud?'

'How else can you hear the music in the words? Close your eyes. Imagine you are blind. What could you tell from the sound of those waves?'

'That it's a calm day?'

'And if it was stormy?'

'The waves would be louder?'

'Give the dog a bone! You must listen to the rhythm of what you've written if you want to manipulate the beat of a human heart. Your story has only long sentences, so the reader's heart beats slowly. To make it quicken, you need short ones. And think about the words you use. A sentence should sound like the thing it is describing. Wind whines and whines the shingle, the crazy pierstakes groan... '

By the time the old gentleman had finished his editing, Rufus's unfinished story had come to look like a colourful spider's web. The old gentleman handed him the copybook. 'Look about your feet,' he said, his tone softening. 'What do you see?'

'Pebbles,' said Rufus. 'Just pebbles.'

'Pick one, Rufus. Out of that grumus of seapebbles pick just one.'

Rufus looked at the pebbles about his feet and chose a small round black one.

'Now hold it to your cheek,' the old gentleman commanded. 'What do you notice?'

'Hard... cold... and smooth'

'Give it here,' commanded the old gentleman. 'Now go find a rough one.'

There were pebbles everywhere, but nothing rough, apart from a tiny piece of concrete that had fallen off the tower. Expanding his search, Rufus ambled sulkily towards the sea.

The closer Rufus got to the waves, the smaller and smoother the pebbles became. They were like tiny storm clouds, and every shade from a bluish-grey to jet black. But all, without exception, were smooth.

At length, close the black rocks, his eyes lit upon a small brown stone with a jagged edge. It wasn't like any of the others and looked as if it didn't quite belong there. He took it back to the old gentleman who snatched it from Rufus and held it in the opposite hand to the smooth pebble Rufus had given him earlier.

'Which did you like best?' he asked, holding out both of his palms.

'The smooth one,' said Rufus.

'Are you sure?'

'Positive.'

'Clever boy! Now take it home and sleep on it. Let Minerva work her magic.'

Rufus loved those mornings when it was just him and his mother; when the twins were sleeping and the room smelled of coffee and toast. It reminded him of how things used to be.

Susan loved those moments too, and would often dawdle over her coffee, putting off waking the twins until the last possible moment. It was the only time when Rufus saw her happy. In the evenings, her quiet moments always seemed less hopeful.

That morning, as Susan watched Rufus eating, she noticed he was taking an age over his cereal. She didn't want to be one of those hovering mothers who never gave children the space to grow. But a withdrawn child was not something any parent could take lightly.

'Those boys bothering you again?' she probed.

'No,' said Rufus cautiously. 'Well, maybe a little.'

'I'll talk to Mrs Stern,' said his mother, packing the twins' lunch boxes into their satchels.

'No, Mom, don't,' said Rufus, suddenly alert. 'You'll only make things worse. I'll tell you if it gets bad. I promise.'

'If you're sure then?' she sighed doubtfully. 'But they shouldn't be...'

'It's OK Mom, honest.'

'You'd tell me, wouldn't you, if something was...'

'Mom?' said Rufus, cutting quickly across her. 'Why are pebbles smooth?'

Rufus had slept for two days with the pebble under his pillow, half-expecting an ending to his story to just come to him in his sleep. But nothing had happened.

'Not all pebbles are smooth,' said Susan as she put her porridge in the microwave.

'The ones at the beach are,' said Rufus.

'That's because the tide washes over them time and time again, wearing them down until they get smoother and smaller.'

'Until there's nothing left?'

'Possibly. A bit like your questions!'

'Very funny!' groaned Rufus.

It had been years since his mother had joked with him like that. He hadn't realised how much he'd missed it until now.

During morning playtime, Rufus was thinking about pebbles and tides and how it must have taken millions of years of washing back and forth to make something so hard feel so smooth. Perhaps that was what the old gentleman had meant: that it took a lot of work to polish something rough; that he had to keep going over his story, correcting and improving, again and again, until it was smooth. Convinced he'd solved yet another of the old gentleman's riddles, he allowed a smile of triumph to cross his face.

'What has you so happy?' said Monika quickly.

'Yeah what?' added Nipper.

Though not really friends, at least not yet, Nipper and Monika had found a common cause in Rufus and had begun to ensure that he was never alone during breaks. They knew that Francie and Tomás would never bother him while he was with a group. Like most bullies, they were essentially cowards.

'Nothing,' mumbled Rufus. 'Just something

I thought of.'

'For your story?' said Monika.

'Kind of.'

'Can I read it?'

'Maybe, when it's finished.'

It was then the thought struck him. How would he know when it was finished? How did writers ever know when to let go of a story, because it seemed to him that there were always more improvements waiting to be revealed?

During lunch break, Monika spotted Rufus standing deep in thought and oblivious to the approach of Francie and Tomás. Protectively, she raced towards him and invited him to join in a chasing game called 'build-up'. It reminded him that not so long ago nobody would have dreamed of asking him to play. In an instant, he had his ending.

'In a minute,' he said.

He raced back to the classroom, opened the

back of his English copybook, and hastily scribbled:

Edward had been invisible for so long he'd become a non-person. Without a body to speak through he'd also become silent. He realised now that he wanted to be seen, heard and listened to.

He wished he had never started chewing those leaves. He had never really wanted to be invisible. What he had wanted all along were friends of his own.

No sooner had Edward realised all that, than the cloak of invisibility began to weaken, and then, finally, to break. It was as if the cloak needed his co-operation to work. Once the desire to be invisible disappeared, so too did the cloak.

'Fitting in these days?' the old gentleman asked.

'No more'n usual,' answered Rufus.

'Good boy!' said the old gentleman. 'Better a cork on the ocean than a cork in a bottle eh? Never let other people's expectations hold you back. Be yourself. And sod the begrudgers!'

Every time it was the same routine: the old gentleman probing the intimacies of his life, but never sharing anything of his own in return. Perhaps, thought Rufus, he also had something to hide, something dark and private.

'Why are you always here?' asked Rufus. 'How come I never see you anywhere else?'

'Why?' the old gentleman laughed. 'Because I've been everywhere else. Because West is forward, East is back, North is white, and South is black.'

'That doesn't make sense,' Rufus protested.

'Not to you, maybe.'

'Not to anyone.'

'But I'm not just *anyone*, am I? And neither

are you. Has no one ever told you that? Are your parents blind, or just stupid?'

'Neither,' sighed Rufus. 'Mum's just too busy, and Dad's... gone.'

'Ah!' the old gentleman triumphed. 'A ghost, a ghouly ghost! I knew it. Haunts you, does he, this spectre?'

'He's not a ghost,' Rufus blurted. 'He's still alive.'

The old man had done it again, deflecting a question with a question, revealing nothing about himself and nimbly manoeuvering Rufus into a revelation of his own.

'But he's in your head.' the old gentleman persisted. 'No?'

Rufus tried to gather himself. 'I think about him sometimes, 's all.'

'Oh, I think you do more than that, son,' the old man continued. 'Wouldn't be sitting here if you had *him* to go to, would we?'

A lump gathered in the back of Rufus' throat

and his eyes began to swell.

'Drink was it?' said the old gentleman.

'Sometimes,' mumbled Rufus, his voice beginning to quaver.

'Take a pew,' said the old gentleman patting the ledge. 'I was never a great man for the confession box, but I dare say I can stretch a point. Let us play.'

Unable to tell whether or not he was being mocked, Rufus didn't respond and so the pair just sat there looking forlornly out to sea.

'Did his talking with his fists I suppose?'

'He never hit me,' said Rufus, 'but...'

Suddenly Rufus felt as if a poison was being drawn from his body. He fought the urge to cry, but his body fought back. His eyes pricked and he started to tremble; tears swelling within him at such a rate that his body could no longer contain them.

'Let it out,' said the old man, patting him on the knee, the coldness of his fingers reaching through to the skin.

The sympathetic touch was too much, and Rufus began to sob. Giant shuddering sobs peppered with desperate gasps for air; heavy cleansing sobs he should have cried ages ago but had been too proud to release. Burying his face in his hands he cried his heart out.

'Poor lamb,' said the old man again, patting Rufus on the shoulder. 'Poor lamb.'

When the heaviest sobs had left him, Rufus tried to explain. 'I had to call an ambulance,' he sniffed, 'but they sent the police as well. I couldn't leave her like that, she was…'

'Not your fault,' said the old gentleman.

'Then why does it feel like it is… if only I'd… you know, waited, then maybe…'

'It's not your fault,' the old gentleman repeated emphatically. 'Only the simplest philadolphus of a fool holds himself responsible for things he cannot control.'

Rufus needed to hear those words, to hear

them over and over so that he could start to believe in them. Until now they had felt like a lame excuse, like the kind of pretence adults use to placate small children. In an instant, the tears stopped.

'Feeling better?' the old man asked as Rufus regained his composure.

'Some,' said Rufus.

'Then listen to me,' said the old man. 'You had no more power over your parents' actions than I had over... Look, make a story of it if you must, but leave the adults to sort out their own lives. You have enough going on in your own.'

'But I suck at stories,' whimpered Rufus.

'And who in allearth's dumbnation told you that?' said the old man. 'Some teacher I'll warrant?'

'No one told me. I just know.'

'Really? Felt the waspish sting of the unflattering word, have we?'

'No, nothing like that. It's just that no matter how often I read what I've written I still can't see what *you* see when you read it.'

Quick as lightening the old gentleman snatched Rufus's wrist and pressed it so violently against the boy's face that Rufus felt his nose smart. For a moment he feared it would bleed.

'Describe your palm,' the old gentleman snapped. 'Every line and scar.'

'I can't see,' winced Rufus. 'It's all blurred.'

Tightening his clasp, the old gentleman pulled Rufus's hand a foot away from his face, his unpared fingernails biting into Rufus's wrist.

'Now what do you see?' he said.

'Fingers,' Rufus gasped. 'Long lines on the palm. Curly ones on the tips of the fingers. Now let go! You're hurting me.'

The old gentleman relaxed his grip and Rufus tore his wrist free from his talons, drawing blood in the process. The scratch stung.

'The best lessons are the most painful,' the old gentleman laughed. 'Hardest to forget. Now tell me, son, what have you learnt from all this?'

'That you're a nutcase,' said Rufus, holding his wrist tightly to stem the blood and numb the pain, 'and I am not your *son*.'

The old gentleman laughed again. 'True, true, very true! But listen to me carefully now, when you get too close to something it's hard to see clearly. Just like the lines on your palm. Understand? Sometimes you have to beetle backwards the better to see.'

Rufus stared at the ground. He was not convinced, and the cut was smarting now.

'Look,' the old man said softly, 'if you hadn't the talent, you would never have known that your story was incomplete. You'd have thought it bloody marvellous. But you couldn't deceive yourself, could you? You knew something wasn't right. You just didn't want to do the work to fix it, so you came looking for help. Am I right or am I left?'

Rufus nodded.

'You have a gift, son. But what you lack is patience and a little experience in the cruel and merciless art of editing. But perhaps I can help you there. Interested?'

'Duh!'

'I'll take that inarticulate grunt as a yes, shall I? You'll have to be bold, mind, and bold as brass. Perhaps even a little reckless.'

'I dunno…'

'Meet me here tonight. After midnight, but before dawn. And come alone, or there'll be blue hell to pay. Understand? Alone.'

'AT NIGHT!' screamed Rufus. 'Mom would never let me out that late.'

'And you always do what your mother tells you, do you? No little secrets? No white lies?

Not even a little one?'

Rufus blushed with embarrassment.

'What a curse o'god state of affairs!' the old gentleman sighed. 'Where's your gumption, child? If you want the gift, be here. Time is running out. I won't offer it twice.'

'But the middle of the night!' Rufus protested. 'Why would you even *want* me to do something like that? I won't do it. I just won't.'

'Yes you will,' said the old man firmly.

'No I won't,' Rufus insisted. 'It's far too dangerous. Why can't you just give it to me now?'

'Because they are all of a piece, the task and the gift: to have one without the other would be meaningless. But you *will* come. You'll risk everything, won't you?'

'Keep it then. I don't need it.'

'Ah Rufus, you know in your heart that isn't true. Even now I can see curiosity swelling like a cancer in your soul. Run along now. You've got some planning to do. And not a word to anyone, mind, not a solitary snakey syllable.'

The twins were squabbling loudly as Rufus returned to the apartment.

'You started it,' Annika screamed.

'Did not,' shrieked Chlöe.

'Did too. You stole my Polly Pocket.'

'Didn't steal it. It's for sharing.'

'MOMMY!' bawled Annika, 'NOT FAIR.'

'OH JUST STOP IT THE TWO OF YOU,' screamed Susan. 'Rufus, put on some cartoons.'

'But Mom! I was going to watch this.'

'Just do it, Rufus. I've had a rough day. Are a few moments of peace and quiet too much to ask?'

It wasn't fair, but Rufus knew from his mother's tone that to answer back would be dangerous. He put on the cartoons and went to his bunk.

For the rest of the evening, Rufus tried to read, but his eyes kept flitting back and forth to the sky outside his window. Ominous looking clouds of ravens were wheeling towards their evening roosts in the trees of Newbridge Demesne. It felt, somehow, like an omen, a warning not to go to the beach.

Over and over he told himself he wouldn't go but, at the same time, he found himself wondering how it might be done. How would he stay awake? What if his mother got up in the night and found him gone? What if the old gentleman wasn't there? What if someone saw him on the road? He wasn't convinced he could do this, and yet...

At about ten o'clock his mother came to bed. The sweet smell on her breath told him she'd had a glass or two of wine. He didn't like to see her drinking and always kept a watchful eye on it. The twins never worried because wine wasn't a 'man drink'. But to Rufus booze was booze. Its presence in the house always made him anxious.

'I never asked,' said Susan, as she came to bed, 'but how did your maths test go today?'

'Easy peasy,' Rufus lied, but Susan was too tired to notice. He was usually asleep by this time, but that fact, too, appeared to have escaped her.

Rufus didn't like lying, but he didn't want his mother to engage him in conversation. He wanted her to pass out like Jonah used to, or for himself to fall asleep so he'd avoid having to face the fact that he was afraid. But neither happened, and the hours dragged by.

Shortly after midnight, his mother began to snore. He wouldn't be getting any sleep for ages now anyway, and so, kicking back the duvet, he climbed quietly down from his bunk, trying not to look at her as he rose. She looked so childlike and vulnerable as she slept that it made him feel protective of her and that, too, filled him with guilt.

The silence in the living room unsettled him. The wall clock was ticking. He couldn't remember ever being aware of the sound of it before, and yet now it seemed so loud. The apartment seemed suddenly strange and unfamiliar.

He found his trainers without stumbling in the dark but didn't bother looking for his socks, or any other clothes for that matter. The quicker he was out, he reasoned, the quicker he'd be back. Checking that his keys were still in the pocket he threw a hoodie over his pyjamas and gingerly opened the apartment door. As he squeezed it shut, he heard a toilet flush in the apartment below.

He waited and listened, his heart pounding in his chest. It took several minutes to convince himself that no one was coming but, once he had, he moved swiftly. As he unlocked his bike a cat knocked over a bottle at the recycling bins. It made him jump. He half-expected someone to investigate, but no one did. His luck was holding.

The area around the Martello tower was dimly lit by the lights of the adjacent hotel. Nevertheless, Rufus felt vulnerable being out alone on a dark night, freezing in a stinging northerly wind, his every breath turning immediately to clouds right in front of his face.

Three times he walked around the tower, searching for the old gentleman, and three times he failed to find him. All he wanted was to complete his challenge and get safely home. In his anxiety, he never noticed that the tower door was slightly ajar or that the chains were hanging loose.

As the sweat beneath his pyjamas began to cool a sense of terror slowly swelled within him. Anything could happen to him out here in the dark, and no one would ever see or hear it.

It wasn't the old gentleman that was crazy, he thought suddenly, it was him!

He scanned the beach one last time but could see nothing in the dark. He listened for the slightest sound but could hear only the wind and the waves. In the far distance, he could see the lights on Howth Head and, from somewhere further away, the pulsing beam of a lighthouse. He could even see a faint blue light coming from the direction of the harbour on Lambay Island. What he could not see, or hear, was any evidence of the old gentleman's presence.

His patience exhausted, he grabbed his bike and was about to ride off when he caught the whiff of a familiar scent. The old gentleman was suddenly behind him, emerging from the shadows on the dark side of the tower, still wearing his round dark glasses.

'Where'd you come from?' whispered Rufus nervously. 'Are you staying at the hotel?'

'Me?' the old gentleman laughed ironically. 'Snug in the premises sumptuous? Don't make me laugh.'

'Well?' said Rufus. 'Did you bring it?'

'Bring what?'

'Whatever you got me out here for?'

'Ah!' the old man exclaimed. 'The pen!'

'A PEN!' gasped Rufus. 'You got me up in the middle of the night to give me a freakin' PEN! I've got loads of pens.'

'Not like this one you don't. Tell me, son, do you know what day it is?'

'Monday?' said Rufus. 'No, it's Tuesday now.'

'And the date?'

'I don't know… June sixteenth?'

'And?'

'And what?'

The old gentleman placed a conspiratorial arm around Rufus's shoulder and guided him to the ledge in front of the tower, away from the lights, and view of the hotel. Rufus's anxiety heightened. He shifted his weight under the old gentleman's grip as if in preparation for escape, but the old gentleman just drew him closer.

'Don't they teach you anything at school?' the old gentleman tutted, his grip tightening. Their bodies were touching tightly, but there was no warmth in the contact. If anything, Rufus felt colder.

'Well?' said the old gentleman impatiently.

'Well what?' said Rufus, starting to shiver.

'The date, child,' snapped the old gentleman. 'Don't you know what day it is?'

Rufus shook his head.

'Blooooooomsday,' said the old gentleman. 'It's Blooooooooooomsday!'

'Never heard of it,' said Rufus, suddenly anxious to get home. The old gentleman was getting louder. Someone was bound to hear.

'Saints alive!' cried the old gentleman incredulously. 'You've never heard of Joyce?

Mr James Joyce, the greatest writer this little island ever produced? Bloomsday is Jem's day, and it is on this day each year that his magic is rekindled. Let him into your soul, boy, and he'll speak through you, as he once spoke through me.'

The old man relaxed his grip and Rufus had almost squirmed free when the old gentleman reached into his inside pocket. Letting go of Rufus he proceeded to un-sheath something as though it were a knife.

Something glistened in the moonlight. A nib. Rufus relaxed. It was just the pen, an old fountain pen. The nib reminded Rufus of an earwig's pincers.

'This,' the old gentleman declared solemnly, 'is the pen that wrote Finnegan's Wake. A girl I once knew was in Paris at the start of the war when an impatient landlord sold off the contents of an abandoned apartment. Here, hold it gently. Place your fingers where the master once placed his.'

Rufus placed the pen between his forefinger and thumb as if about to write. It felt the same as anything might feel in fingers that were numb with cold. But he liked the thought of owning an antique; a pen different from all the other pens in his class.

Turning away, the old gentleman began to recite. 'His own identity was fading out into a grey impalpable world...'

There was something tragic in the old man's tone, but Rufus wasn't listening. He was lost in the type of practical concerns that are second nature to every child raised in a household forever short of money.

'What happens when the ink runs out?' he asked suddenly.

'What?'

'The ink. What do I do when it runs out?'

'By that time,' said the old gentleman, 'you'll no longer need it. Now leave me be. Run along before you're missed.'

Rufus got up to go; then stopped dead in his tracks.

'I don't know your name,' he said.

'O'Reilly,' the old gentleman answered, tipping his hat in an old-fashioned manner. 'Persse O'Reilly. That's P, E, R, double S, E. Not Percy, just Persse. Plain and simple. Rhymes with verse.'

'That's a funny name,' said Rufus, taking a sly pleasure in the fact.

'You can talk, you little pup!' the old gentleman growled as he gave Rufus a playful cuff on the back of the head. 'And it took you long enough to ask! Off home with you now, before the mistress discovers you've slipped the leash.'

Rufus yawned his way through school the following day, worrying incessantly about the pen. Unable to find his schoolbag in the dark the previous night, he had hidden the pen inside one of his Wellington boots. But the following morning he was last to the breakfast table and, not daring to advertise his deceit, he had been left with no choice but to leave the pen in the boot and would spend the day in dread of the twins finding it.

At school that day, Rufus decided to look up James Joyce on the computer. The entry was brief:

James Augustine Aloysius Joyce (born Dublin, Ireland, 2nd February 1882 – died Zürich, Switzerland, 13th January 1941), an Irish novelist famous for his experimental use of language.

His attention was quickly diverted to the accompanying photograph. It was Persse, or as near as made no difference! The clothes were identical, as were the hat and cane. The face, too, could have been Persse's, except that Rufus had never seen his eyes and Persse was much older than the man in the photograph.

Could Persse be Joyce? He looked again at the opening sentence. It was impossible! Joyce had been dead for sixty-eight years! So then, who exactly was Persse O'Reilly? And why was he always dressed like James Joyce?

Rufus pondered the possibility of Persse being a ghost, but then remembered how Persse had touched him: the friendly pat on the knee, the painful grip on the wrist, the way he'd pulled him close on the night he'd given him the pen. He was most definitely a creature of flesh and blood.

On his return from school that day Rufus found the apartment empty. Retrieving the pen from its hiding place he opened his copybook, sat down on the sofa, and waited for inspiration. Logic told him he was wasting his time, but a part of him wanted to test the old gentleman's promises.

He sat there for ages, listening to the wall clock measuring the silence, wondering if this was just another of the old gentleman's riddles, all but forgetting that he still had the pen in his hand. Then suddenly, as he began to flick through his old stories, he felt a sudden and irresistible urge to correct.

Before he knew it, he was crossing out words and replacing them with better ones, breaking long sentences into shorter ones and merging short sentences into longer ones. He got so caught up in this flurry of activity that he barely noticed the time passing, or that the ink that flowed from his nib was neither black nor blue, but red. Blood red! Flowing from the nib like a severed vein.

And the ink wasn't the only thing he'd failed to notice. The apartment door had swung open and the twins were hurtling in, followed by Susan, bone-tired and frayed, stumbling under the weight of her shopping.

'Whatcha doing?' asked Annika.

'Nothing,' said Rufus, as Susan shrugged off her coat and kicked off her shoes.

'Lemme see,' said Chlöe.

'NO!' snapped Rufus. He tried to hide what he was doing, but it was too late.

'MOM-MY!' cried Chlöe in her best tattle-tale voice. 'Rufus's pen is bleeding.'

Rufus scowled at Annika, but before she could react, his mother was on top of him.

'Where did you get this?'

'Persse gave it to me.'

'Who's Persse?'

And so it began, the biggest row that Rufus had ever had with his mother.

'If he's laid a hand on you…'

'He never touched me.'

'And that name. What is it? French? Latin? How could you be so stupid?'

The more Rufus tried to defend his

relationship with the old gentleman, the louder and more hysterical his mother became. She screamed so violently that she frightened the twins, who scuttled away to the bedroom to sit in fretful silence, their little fingers plugging their ears.

'We didn't do anything wrong,' cried Rufus. 'Nothing happened. All we do is talk.'

'Nothing happened! You're having secret meetings with a strange man for heaven's sake; a man who has been grooming you for who knows what! Don't you realise the risks you were taking? What has gotten into you? How could you be so stupid? You're just like your father; wrapped in your own little cocoon!'

'You don't understand,' cried Rufus. 'He's just an old man and all we do is talk.'

'Talk! About what?'

'About writing.'

'So that's how all this started. Well for a start, that's going to stop.'

'No, it's not. You can't make me.'

'I can, and I will,' cried his mother, her nostrils flaring. 'You're not leaving my sight until…'

'That's not fair,' Rufus broke in. 'I didn't do anything wrong… Jonah would understand.'

'There's a hell of a difference between understanding and caring. I'm the one that's here. Get it! Don't you EVER forget that. You hear me? I'm here, and he's not. He's the one that ran out on you, not me.'

'IT WASN'T MY FAULT HE LEFT!' screamed Rufus. 'IT WASN'T ME THAT WAS ALWAYS PICKING ON HIM.'

Susan felt his words like a blow to the head. Rufus had never been deliberately hurtful before. It was more than she could bear. For one brief moment she hated him; hated him for looking like his father; hated him for telling the truth. A look of revulsion crossed her face: a look that could no more be taken back than

Rufus's scalding words.

'OH GO TO BED, YOU HATEFUL CHILD!' she screamed, raising an open hand as if to slap him, but stopping short of his face. 'AND GIVE ME THAT PEN.'

Back in the bedroom, Rufus could hear his mother sobbing as she set about washing the dishes. At one point in the general clatter of crockery, he heard a cupboard door slam, and then silence.

He wished his mother would turn on the television so that he would have something other than the silence to listen to. He prayed that he would fall asleep before she came to bed. He had crossed a line and he knew it. Maybe Persse was right; maybe he *was* more like Jonah than he knew.

Standing at the kitchen sink, Susan pondered her reaction. Even Jonah, in his drunkenness, had never raised a hand to the children. He'd only ever taken his anger out on her, as she had on him. But at least she'd had good reason. Jonah had undertaken to be the breadwinner for the family, but it was never supposed to be minimum wage forever. They were both intelligent. They should have had prospects, but Jonah had gotten lazy and lost all ambition. Jonah had left them trapped.

She would never have let things slide like that. *She* would have fought like a tiger for a promotion, for a better job, for her children's future. But then it dawned on her. Even as a runner Jonah had been totally unambitious. He had never pretended otherwise. Oh, God! How could she have been so blind!

There would be no tea for ages now. The twins were hungry, but they knew better than to leave the bedroom. They would have to wait until later, when Mommy, eyes puffy and face still wet, would summon them for some buttered toast and a glass of milk. After that, it would simply be a matter of waiting for the storm to blow over.

Inevitably, the nightmares returned. Only this time there was to be no comforting hand on the forehead. His mother simply lay there, in angry silence, pretending to be asleep. With Jonah, fights were quickly forgotten, but Susan wasn't Jonah. Not by a long chalk!

Over the course of this difficult period, Rufus neither wrote anything new nor managed to meet up with Persse. But that didn't stop him from composing stories in his head and trying to memorise them.

As for Susan, who no longer felt able to trust Rufus, she was forced to quit her job to keep an eye on him during the summer holidays. The effects were felt immediately in her purse, and on the kitchen table.

Instead of beef or fish, the children now found themselves eating cheaper meats like pork liver or cow's heart. Scrambled eggs became something more than just a breakfast dish, and pork chops, once a favourite of the twins, appeared so regularly on their plates that they grew to hate the sight of them.

But no one ever complained, and Rufus never dared let on that he had figured out that their frequent trips to the playground were a strategy to disguise the fact that meals were being missed. As for clothing, no one dared to mention that a shirt was getting tight or a shoe beginning to pinch.

Nothing had to be said for the twins to understand the family's trouble. They couldn't fail to notice how Rufus was once again stripping wet sheets from his bed each morning; or how neither party to the bust-up could look the other in the eye. They came to hate the suffocating silences that rippled in the wake of words that should never have been spoken and in which every sentence now had to be weighed twice before being joined to another.

'Rufus?' whispered Annika one night after her brother had finished reading the twins their bedtime story. 'What would happen to us if Mommy left?'

'She wouldn't,' said Rufus, less out of belief than a desire to stifle the question.

But the twins were persistent. 'Daddy did,' they whispered.

'That was different,' mumbled Rufus.

'Why?' said Annika.

'Moms don't leave their kids,' Rufus assured them. 'Not even animals.'

Chlöe sat up in her bed. 'But if she did...'

'Then I suppose we'd have to go live with Aunt Lucy,' sighed Rufus impatiently.

'Oh no,' gasped Annika. 'I wouldn't like that. I don't like Aunt Lucy.'

'No one is going anywhere,' whispered Rufus, straining to find a confident tone.

'Promise?' pleaded Chlöe.

Rufus didn't answer. His mother had once

loved Jonah and now she didn't. Nothing, absolutely nothing, was impossible.

'Rufus?' said Annika at length. 'Will you leave us when you and Monika get married?'

'What?' Rufus gasped.

'Ania said Monika's your girlfriend,' Annika persisted. 'And boyfriends and girlfriends get married and have babies and houses,' Chlöe giggled.

'She's not my girlfriend,' Rufus protested. 'And anyway, only adults get married.'

'But what if...' Annika began.

'Enough already!' snapped Rufus. 'I told you, nobody's going anywhere. Go to sleep.'

Over the following nights these 'what if' conversations became something of a routine. Mostly they revolved around the potential consequences of their mother leaving, though occasionally they'd drift into wondering what would happen if their father actually came back.

Would he return as Charming Daddy, or Funny Daddy, as the Daddy they secretly loved and felt guilty for missing? Or would he return as the Daddy who hit Mommy and then ran away? They ached for Normal, in every sense of the word.

A spell of exceptional weather arrived like a hasty apology for the late arrival of summer. Temperatures soared from the high teens to the low thirties, and sunhats and sunglasses were finally recalled from their winter resting places. But, fearing that the old gentleman might still be about, Susan refused to bring the children anywhere near the beach.

Inevitably, Rufus got bored. He couldn't even call on his friends. Monika was at a chamber music camp in Cork and Nipper was attending a soccer camp that Susan couldn't afford. And so Rufus spent his days revisiting books he'd already read, or sitting by his bedroom window watching the trains pass.

Then, one sunny day, Susan's mood lightened. She decided to treat the children to a tour of the farm at Newbridge House. The house had once been the home of the Protestant Archbishop of Dublin, Charles Cobbe. They had learnt about the Cobbes in school, but neither the house nor the farm had ever held much interest for Rufus beyond what he could see from the outside.

The twins, on the other hand, never tired of the farm. They raced to the incubator to see if any chicks were hatching. Ignoring their excitement, Rufus kept walking, lost in thought.

A short while later, finding himself alone, Rufus settled himself under a chestnut tree to wait for the others to catch up. A tiny cave had been formed by the roots of the tree and inside he noticed two oval-shaped stones sitting on a bed of moss, like eggs in a nest.

'Now what are you doing here?' he wondered aloud, taking out the stones to examine them.

The stones were a silvery shade of grey but, apart from the colour, were unremarkable. And yet, he thought, someone must have put them there, and in that odd configuration, for a reason. He sat back against the tree and closed his eyes.

He took up a stone and started to finger it. It felt as smooth as glass and seemed to get warmer the more he stroked it. Then he began to hear it: a faint humming sound. It seemed quite musical. He looked around to see if anyone else could hear it, but no one appeared to. It was as if the sound was not playing around him, but through him.

He put down the stone and the music stopped: picked it up and it began again. The longer he held it, the louder it got. It was an odd sort of music: a kind he'd never heard before. And it was strangely soothing. He started to hum along with it. That was when it started to happen...

'RU-FUS?'

His mother's peace-wrecking bellow woke him with a start. Rufus stood up and dropped the stone. He resented being called from his daydreams; hated leaving a story unfinished.

'There you are,' said Susan, her tone softening. 'Didn't you hear me calling you? Here! Take this ice cream from me before it drips all over my dress. What on earth possessed you to run off like that?'

'Nothing,' he said sourly.

'Look,' said Susan, 'I know you're bored. We'll head back to the playground for a bit to let the twins run off their excess energy, and then we'll head straight home. Promise.'

The conciliatory tone took Rufus by surprise. He wondered if it was the start of a thaw in the cold war that had existed between them since the night she confiscated the pen. Something had changed, that was for sure. He looked briefly at the stone he had just dropped and wondered... then dismissed the idea as ridiculous.

Back at the playground, in a ploy to escape the twins, he started a game of hide-and-seek, then climbed over the iron fence to hide in the bushes behind the bench where his mother was sitting.

'The girls weren't planned,' Susan was explaining to an old woman he'd never seen before, 'and it became impossible to go back to college after they were born.'

The old woman smiled knowingly. 'You never get the life you expect,' she said, with what Rufus took to be a Scottish accent. 'But that can be part of the excitement, can't it? You don't regret having those beautiful bairns now, do you?'

'Oh, there are days!' laughed Susan. 'But you're right. I'd be lost without them. Perhaps if we'd had some parental support we might have managed, but both sides disapproved.'

'Mixed marriage was it?'

'His parents were Mormon; my father staunchly Catholic. Neither side was happy. The phone never stopped ringing. It got to the point where it was easier to cut off contact altogether. Guess we let things slide after that. Christmas cards and birthday cards, that was about the extent of it.'

Rufus had pieced the story together over the years: how Jonah had been studying geology when he'd had to drop out of college and take a job as an unskilled labourer in a car factory; how Susan had been studying English literature when she, too, had to abandon her scholarship and become a stay-at-home mom; how they both had always planned to go back to college one day, until the arrival of the twins had killed that dream stone-dead.

What Rufus didn't know, and struggled to understand, was why his mother was suddenly confessing her life story to a stranger.

'But the children,' the old woman said at length, 'they helped to heal things, no?'

'Not really,' said Susan matter-of-factly. 'My mother died when I was three and my father three years after my eldest was born. He could have come to me, I suppose. He could afford to travel, and I couldn't. But we were each as stubborn as the other, I guess. This is the first I've been home since I left.'

'You never got to his funeral?'

'Couldn't afford to,' said Susan. 'I don't think my sister has ever forgiven me. But to be fair, she's been good to us these last months. After Jonah put me in the hospital I had to do something drastic, and she...'

'Hospital? Oh, my dear, I'm so sorry. I didn't realise. It must be so painful talking about something like that and here's me…'

'No, it's okay,' Susan reassured her. 'It's a lot easier when it's behind you.'

'Aye, time is a great healer, so they say.'

'Perhaps. And yet, in some ways, it would have been easier if he'd died.'

Rufus bit his lip. He dearly wished that he hadn't heard that. There are some things that once heard cannot be unheard. They change everything. He wanted to protest but was too afraid to reveal himself. He'd left it too late, and worse was to come.

'Don't get me wrong,' Susan rushed to add. 'I'm not yearning to dance on his grave or anything. It just would have been easier, less complicated all round.'

'You don't mean that?' the old woman gasped incredulously. 'Surely not!'

'Don't I? Well, maybe not. But I get so tired of having to deflect the kids' questions.'

'Only natural they should miss him. There's

no hope of reconciliation then? He hasn't turned his life around? For the sake of the bairns?'

'I've no idea what he's doing. I just know that he won't come near us again. I was tired of having to make lame excuses about falling down the stairs or walking into a cupboard door; of having to cover the bruises with heavy make-up or long-sleeved blouses; of taking pleasure in other people's failed marriages just so I could pretend that mine wasn't so bad. So I pressed charges.'

'Oh dear,' said the old woman, looking increasingly uncomfortable. 'You've certainly been through a lot.'

'I should have acted earlier, I suppose, but lying in that hospital bed I realised that divorce wasn't the worst that could happen. Class A Misdemeanour, they said. So if he shows his face again he'll be arrested. A year in county jail might help him get his life back in order, but we're finished as a family. There's no need for him to feel trapped anymore.'

'Oh, my poor dear,' the old woman repeated as she got up to leave. 'I really am so sorry. I hope things work out for you.'

Sometimes being invisible sucked: sometimes you heard things that left you feeling cursed, and deservedly so. Rufus felt angry at his mother and sorry for her at the same time. He felt angry at his father, and sorry for him too. Most of all he felt sorry for himself, for being caught between the two. If only he hadn't made that call. If only he hadn't eavesdropped on his mother. If only…

At that moment Rufus was seized with a rebellious thought. He had, he now believed, earned the right to his own secrets. And so, despite his mother's prohibition, he resolved to continue to create his own stories. If he couldn't write them down, then he would keep them fresh by telling them to the twins. He would start that very night. Instead of reading a bedtime story, he would recite his latest creation: the story of 'The Singing Stones.'

At the beginning of August, Monika returned from music camp. She was walking with her mother and sister to the playground in Newbridge House when she spotted Rufus dawdling on the steps to the manor house.

'Rufus!' she screeched. 'Haven't seen you in ages. What have you been up to?'

It had only been a couple of months, but Monika looked different. She had on a tightly fitting top that accentuated her feminine curves and was wearing mascara and a light pink shade of lipstick.

'Nothing much,' he sighed, trying hard not to stare. 'I've been grounded.'

'How long for?' asked Monika, brushing a hair from her forehead.

Monika seemed older somehow, and more

delicate in her movements. Even her hair seemed different; no longer worn in plaits or ponytails but hanging loose, like a silken waterfall. He could smell its lemony fragrance as the breeze snatched at it.

Rufus had never really seen Monika as a girl before. She had always been just Monika. It unsettled him a little.

'All summer,' he mumbled.

Monika waved her mother and sister away, indicating that she'd catch up with them. 'All Summer!' she gasped. 'Are you serious? What did you do? Was it really bad?'

'Not really,' sighed Rufus. 'I was just meeting someone who was teaching me to write.'

'You mean like a summer camp?'

'Kind of, except it was just me.'

'What's so bad about that?'

'I didn't tell her, s'all.'

Rufus began to babble. He told Monika all

about his midnight trip to the beach, and about the antique pen (omitting any mention of special powers).

'Deadly!' exclaimed Monika. 'Weren't you scared?'

'Not really. Just sort'a did it.'

'At music camp, some of us would sneak out at night to raid the kitchen for a midnight feast, but it wasn't nearly as adventurous as that, and all we ever found were digestive biscuits. Was your mother furious?'

'She doesn't know about the night thing,' said Rufus. 'You have to swear not to tell.'

'Okay. If you say so. But you must be the bravest or stupidest boy in school. Anything could have happened to you!'

'Don't *you* start! Persse isn't like that. I just wish I could have told him why I had to stop coming. There's loads I wanted to tell him.'

'You've got news?'

'I found out something. A secret.'

'Secrets! Oh, please tell.'

'Family thing. Can't talk about it.'

'You mean with me? You seem willing enough to discuss it with a strange old man. Are we not friends anymore?'

'Yes but...'

'Never mind. Keep your secret.'

The instant Monika got up to leave Rufus felt seized by a premonition of loss.

'She went to the cops,' he blurted after her. 'That's why he never came back.'

Monika stopped and turned.

'Your friend at the beach?'

'No, my Dad. Mom filed charges. He hit her. Put her in hospital. He was drunk.'

Monika retraced her steps. 'Oh Rufus, that's... I don't know what to say. Shove over. Make room.'

Shoulder to shoulder they sat in silence, arms touching but not moving, aware of the heat of each other's bodies in a way that was unfamiliar to them both.

'Why'd she have to do that?' asked Rufus at length. 'Why couldn't she have simply got a divorce? Lots of parents get divorced and the kids still get to see both.'

Monika rested a consoling hand weightlessly on his shoulder. 'I don't know,' she said tenderly. 'Maybe she was afraid. Why don't you ask her?'

'Are you kidding me?'

'Really? Then how did you find out.'

'I overheard her.'

'Talking about it? Who with?'

'Some woman she met on a park bench. I was hiding from the twins when she started telling this old Scottish woman all about it.'

'So, she felt easier confiding in a stranger?'

'I suppose.'

Monika smiled and shook her head. 'Like mother, like son,' she said.

Despite himself, Rufus smiled back.

'Come on,' said Monika, reaching for his hand. 'Race you to the swings.'

As Monika attempted to pull him to his feet Rufus resisted. She had taken hold of his hand and never had something so awkward felt so important. But then she let it go, and it was as if it had never happened. He tried to act cool, as if it was of little consequence. But it was.

It was different with Monika than with Nipper. But she was just a friend, he told himself, a friend who just happened to be a girl; a girl he wanted to be more his friend than Nipper's; a girl who had suddenly taken to attracting his attention in school by touching his arm and resting a lazy hand on his shoulder whenever they were chatting in a group.

Monika so engaged Rufus's thoughts that morning that he completely forgot that it was his birthday. He didn't remember until later that evening when his mother pulled a cake and candles from its hiding place in the oven and had the twins sing happy birthday to him. They all laughed at his blushes. Had it been a year already!

For his birthday Susan gave Rufus a book token for thirty euro and a hardback notebook in which to write his stories. 'Just promise me that you won't neglect your studies,' she said as she gave it to him, 'and that you'll stay away from the beach unless you're with someone.'

It wasn't exactly forgiveness, but to Rufus it was as near as made no difference. For the first time in weeks, he felt comfortable at home. He still nurtured the hope that he hadn't seen the last of Persse but, for the time being, he was more concerned with getting his stories down on paper.

In no time at all Rufus finished the stories of 'The Singing Stones', 'The Telepathic Jellyfish', 'The Starfish that fell from the Sky', 'The Adventures of Sniffer the Seal' and his latest, 'Waiting for Napoleon', a story about a young gunner serving at the Martello Tower in Donabate, who passes the long night watches making up stories to tell his comrades.

He was also close to finishing a story he called 'Lost in Time' – the tale of a young Polish girl who gets caught in a strong current while swimming off Tower Bay, starts to drown, and wakes up on the same beach, one hundred years into the future.

Most of his stories were pure fantasy, containing very in the way of personal reflection or experience. There was one story, however, that was different from all the rest. It told the tale of a young baseball player from a broken home.

Within this story, Rufus had woven memories of his father and, in the writing of it, he had discovered something important. The page always listened. The page was never too busy. Bad memories didn't hurt quite so much on the page.

Over the following days, as his birthday notebook began to fill, the story that mattered most to him, the very first story that he had attempted to write, remained frustratingly unfinished. Something was missing, something vital, and its absence gnawed away at him like a phantom pain.

Unable to ask Persse's advice, Rufus began to wonder if the pen could help. But to Susan, that confiscated pen had a sinister aura about it. She couldn't decide if the old gentleman had simply been generous, or if he had been grooming her son for something unspeakable.

More than once Susan came close to throwing the pen out but, in the end, she had hidden it in a jar on the top shelf of the kitchenette. If it really *had* belonged to James Joyce, she reasoned, then it might be worth a small fortune someday.

Without the pen, however, Rufus felt like a

sailor lost at sea. He was desperate to finish that story. Truly desperate. But that particular horizon remained tantalisingly out of reach.

All too soon school had re-started, Susan had returned to work, and a new mentor had entered Rufus's life – a fresh-faced young woman with silky auburn hair that reached to the small of her back.

Caroline Goode was a lot younger than the other teachers at Darwin Co-educational, and a lot prettier. She smelled of lilac and never raised her voice. She kept everyone's attention by giving them hers. There wasn't a single one of her students that couldn't be spurred to greater effort by one of her smiles.

It didn't take Miss Goode long to discover that Rufus was advanced in his use of language. Where other children might use a word such as *small* or *tiny*, Rufus would use *diminutive*; instead of *angelic* he would write *seraphic*. He was trying hard, maybe too hard. Sometimes the simpler word worked best.

A lot of the credit for his improving literary skills, Rufus suspected, belonged to the pen that his mother had finally returned to him. The pen didn't give him ideas for stories – he had to come up with those himself. He only ever picked up the pen when he wanted to edit. But once he did, he began to imagine that Joyce himself was reading his stories and telling him where they were weak. He would then feel compelled to re-shape them; to place the right word in the right place at the right time.

Often, after the pen had done its work, the pages would be covered in red ink and Rufus would have to begin again from scratch. Sometimes the pen would cross out entire paragraphs of which he had been especially proud, but were of little use as they took actually something *away* from the story.

The first draft of each story was always the worst, and Rufus had come to accept that the pen would be merciless. But he tolerated the attacks of red ink because he understood that without that first weak effort there could never be a second, and without the second there could never be a third, and so on, until he finally had a version that the pen wouldn't want to change.

All of this was fine when Rufus was writing for himself, but not when he was writing to a deadline, and so he never, ever, let the pen loose on his homework. Sometimes perfection wasn't practical.

But it wasn't just the pen that was guiding Rufus. Miss Goode was helping too. One day she asked the class to write a short essay about spring and Rufus wrote two pages describing the morning sun as it spread across the frosted fields in front of Newbridge House. It reminded Miss Goode of a chapter in a book she was reading and so she asked Rufus to remain behind during morning playtime.

'I'd like to you to read over what you've written here,' she said warmly.

'Why?' said Rufus. 'Is something wrong?'

'Not at all,' said Miss Goode. 'No, I just want to refresh your memory before I show you something.'

It took about three minutes for Rufus to review his essay, after which Miss Goode reached into her handbag and pulled out a paperback copy of *On the Black Hill* by Bruce Chatwin. A dog-eared page marked the start of chapter twenty-nine.

'Read the first sentence, Rufus' said Miss Goode. 'Just the first, mind.'

'Spring,' read Rufus, 'had dusted the larches.'

For a moment the pair sat in silence, allowing the frosted imagery to sink in. He could scarcely believe it. Chatwin had accomplished in just five words what he'd just spent two pages trying to describe.

'Oh, Miss, that's brilliant!' he gushed.

'I'm glad you think so, because I do too,' said Miss Goode. 'Look, here's another of my favourites.'

She took a larger book from her drawer and drew his attention to a sentence underlined in pencil.

'Paris rawly waking,' Rufus read aloud, 'crude sunlight on her lemon streets.' Pausing on the last word he looked to Miss Goode. 'Who?' he asked.

'Joyce,' said Miss Goode, smiling. 'Who else could it be, but James Joyce?'

Rufus's jaw dropped. He was tempted to tell her everything there and then, before remembering what had happened the last time he had told an adult about Persse O'Reilly. For the rest of morning break, however, he couldn't help remembering Persse and playing in his head with the sound of the magical words he'd just read.

'Spring dusted larches,' he mumbled softly, 'crude sunlight and lemon streets. Bring crusted partridge, cold moonlight, and lemon sweets!'

As he passed the vegetable patch, Daisy Godwin, overheard him talking strangely to himself. 'What did I tell you?' she sneered to her little entourage. 'There's definitely something wrong with him. He totally creeps me out!'

Thinking a bit of creative writing might do wonders for children, Miss Goode, approached Mrs Stern the following day with a proposal. She wanted to run a short story competition that would be open to all ages.

'You've thought this one through, have you?' teased Mrs Stern.

'I think it would be good for them,' Miss Goode persisted. 'It's hard to get them excited about writing if they simply view it as homework.'

'Let me think about it,' said Mrs Stern. We wouldn't want a repeat of the European Food Fair fiasco, now, would we?'

Miss Goode's face reddened. On the last day of her first week as a teacher in the school, Caroline Goode had decided to enliven her geography lesson by getting the kids to organise a European Food Fair. Each child was asked to draw the name of a major European country out of a hat and to try to locate something edible from that country over the weekend.

But when Monday came, she wished she had been more specific. The entire class had brought in chocolate: Irish, Belgian, German, Swedish, Swiss, Spanish. You name it, they'd found it. And all in contravention of the school's healthy eating policy. From the smile Monika shot in his direction, Miss Goode concluded that the brains behind the prank had been Nipper McVicar.

Having had her fun with Miss Goode, Mrs Stern agreed to the competition, as long as it was open to the entire school and prizes were given to the best story in each age group. It was a simple story competition, she thought to herself. What could possibly go wrong?

During lunch break that day Monika was humming a tune that Rufus didn't recognise.

'What's that?' he asked.

'Elgar,' said Monika. 'Cello concerto. I'm learning the first movement.'

'Sounds difficult.'

'Duh!'

The conversation faltered after that. Rufus knew nothing about classical music and his lack of knowledge made him feel inadequate.

'God, I'm so tired,' yawned Monika at length.

'I was up half the night texting Dara.'

Dara wasn't a name that Rufus recognised and the possibility that Monika had a boyfriend sent an unexpected current of alarm racing through his body.

'Who's Dara?' he asked.

'Oh, just a friend from music camp,' said Monika playfully.

'What does he play then?' he mumbled.

'Viola,' answered Monika with a smile. 'And *he's* a she. Did you think she was a boy? Oh Rufus, were you jealous? That's so sweet!'

'I wasn't jealous. Just curious,' said Rufus lamely. To spare his blushes, Monika let it pass.

'Are you writing a story for the competition?' she asked, quickly changing the subject.

"You know these stories will be read aloud in class, don't you?' said Rufus. 'It would be asking for trouble.'

'But Rufus you *have* to enter!' Monika

insisted, placing a friendly hand on his arm.

Rufus's blushes deepened. He had decided not to enter for fear of ridicule, but if Monika wanted him to, then that was different. It mattered what Monika thought.

'C'mon Rufus,' she persisted, 'Oh my God! You could use Tomás and Francie as characters.'

'Are you mad?' said Rufus. 'They haven't said a word to me for ages and I'd like to keep it that way. You've no idea how bad it was when I first came here and they…'

'Really? I mean, REALLY?'

'What?'

'Come on Rufus. Seriously? It took me a year to learn enough English to be able to ask to visit the bathroom. For a whole year, I could tell that kids were making fun of me but couldn't understand how. At least you already spoke English.'

'I suppose. I hadn't thought…'

'Look, don't let those idiots stop you. Write or don't write. But don't let *them* be the reason.'

Monika's encouragement roused the competitor in Rufus but, fearing the stories he'd already written would be seized upon as childish, he decided to write a new one: about a boy, an old man, and a tower. And that was the story that Rufus Black eventually handed to Caroline Goode; the story that would alter the course of his life.

'Congratulations, Rufus,' said Mrs Stern, beaming with schoolmarmish approval as she presented him with a twenty-euro book token. 'We loved your story so much that we'd like to enter it for the Primary Schools Short Story Award, if that's OK with you?'

Rufus stared blankly at Mrs Stern.

'Even if you were simply to make the final,' Mrs Stern continued, 'your story would be published in the annual anthology. So, Rufus, what do you say?'

'I don't know,' said Rufus, all manner of questions churning in his head. But before he could properly absorb what exactly it was that he was being asked to do, he had nodded his consent.

He thought little about the competition for weeks after that, but one cold wet morning in early October he found himself summoned to the Fitzroy Room. Named after Robert Fitzroy, captain of *The Beagle* during Darwin's historic voyage to the Galapagos, the Fitzroy Room was little more than a windowless box room, small, cramped, and always too hot. But for now, it was where the school principal had her office.

'Come in Rufus,' said Mrs Stern. 'Take a seat. You've probably guessed why I've sent for you.'

Rufus braced himself for disappointment.

'Well, before I tell you what the judges had to say, I just want to tell you how proud I am, indeed how proud we all are of you. You're a credit to the school. I imagine your parents are very proud of you too.'

It was a careless remark and Rufus shifted uneasily in his seat. He couldn't say that *they* were proud of him, because there was no longer a *they*. He could say that his mother was, but that might invite a follow-up question and he didn't want to go there. Why couldn't she just get on with it, tell him the bad news and let him go?

Observing the anxiety in Rufus's face, Mrs Stern hastened to her point.

'Well, as you may have guessed,' she said flatly, 'the results have arrived. The judges were full of praise for your work, but only twelve stories were selected for the final and, out of all the schools in the Dublin area, not a single story made it... except yours.'

'You mean?'

'Yes, Rufus. You're through to the final.'

'YES!' screamed Rufus, leaping from his chair.

For the first time in his life, Rufus saw Mrs Stern smile: a smile as wide as the Broadmeadow Estuary. Maybe she wasn't so fierce after all.

'You know what this means, don't you Rufus?'

Rufus knew only too well what it meant. His story would be published in a book and his name would be right there beside it. So, if and when Jonah was ever to Google his name, there it would be. In a book! A book Jonah could buy. He would know where they were!

The following Monday, Mrs Stern received an unexpected phone call from a man called Roger Coyle. It was bad news.

'Good God!' she exclaimed. 'What on earth

for.'

'Plagiarism,' said Coyle. 'The organisers were going to write to you, but I've asked them to hold off until I've had a chance to speak with the boy.'

'But how?' said Judith.

'It was the subject matter that was called into question, I'm afraid. It bears a striking similarity to a story that won the prize back in 1996.'

'Really?' said Mrs Stern. 'How extraordinary!'

'You have no idea *how* extraordinary!' said Coyle. 'The only real difference was the setting. The '96 story was set in Sutton.'

'But how could that be?' exclaimed Mrs Stern. 'The boy said it was a memoir. I'm certain his mother can verify that.'

'The whys of the matter are irrelevant at this stage, I'm afraid. The rules are very clear. But if I can clear up the matter of intent, I might just be able to brush it under the carpet, or at the very least allow for an honourable withdrawal.'

'I see,' sighed Mrs Stern distractedly.

'I'm not sure you do,' said Coyle, unsure of Mrs Stern's tone but suspecting her of a defensive and calculating self-interest. 'To be honest, I'm not sure I do myself, but I don't believe the boy is to blame.'

'I wish I could be so certain,' said Mrs Stern. 'He's rather an odd fish. I assume the '96 book is still in print?'

Coyle paused. He felt suddenly protective of the boy. He could almost hear the wheels turning as Mrs Stern's brain began to formulate a damage limitation strategy.

'You could probably still unearth a copy in the libraries,' he said slowly, 'but I don't think that's how this came about. It's rather complicated.'

'His mother will be very upset,' Mrs Stern

continued, barely listening now.

Ever since it opened, the experimental school had been treated with suspicion by many in the village and, as the principal, Mrs Stern always took criticism of her school personally.

'There's no need for anyone to know just yet,' said Coyle with more urgency than was perhaps required.

But Mrs Stern wasn't listening. 'There'll be a scandal of course, for the family, and indeed for the school. I'll have to notify the Board of Management.'

'Please don't,' said Coyle, even more emphatically, 'at least until I've had a chance to speak with the boy. I have an idea of what might be behind this and I'd like a chance to explore the theory before any action is taken. I could call to the school. Would ten o'clock on Wednesday be suitable?'

By an unfortunate quirk of fate, sitting on

the punishment bench outside the Fitzroy Room that morning was Francie McKellit. He had been sent to see the principal for swearing in class. The office door was ajar and Francie had heard everything. He hadn't understood it all, but he'd heard enough.

'Oh!' said Mrs Stern as she opened the office door. 'I'd forgotten you were here. Go tell Mr Thomas I need to speak with him urgently. When you've done that you can return to your class. I'll deal with you later.'

Francie knew that Mrs Stern was sending for Mr Thomas to discuss Rufus. So, having told Mr Thomas he was wanted, Francie pretended to return to class, then doubled back and resumed his place on the punishment bench. He couldn't hear *every* word they said this time, but he heard the title of a book and the allegation that Rufus had copied a story from it.

'We'd better check the school library,' said

Mrs Stern, 'in case we have a copy.'

'I'll check it now,' said Mr Thomas.

Hearing Mr Thomas rise from his seat, Francie raced back to class. His first thought, on hearing of Rufus's disqualification, had been to broadcast the American's disgrace all over the school. But that would have gotten *him* into trouble as well.

But if Mr Thomas was looking for evidence that Rufus had copied his story, then evidence he would have. Mr Thomas would have beaten him to the school library, but the county library...

'Sit down, Rufus,' said Mrs Stern, fixing her quarry with a flinty glare. 'I have a rather grave matter to discuss with you.'

The ominous tone led Rufus to assume he had failed to win the overall prize. But he wasn't overly disappointed. His story would still be published alongside the other twelve finalists. Jonah would still be able to buy the book and he would still see his name in print.

'It's OK,' said Rufus. 'Not everybody can win.'

'Well,' the principal sighed, 'that's what I want to speak to you about. I'm afraid your story has been disqualified.'

Suddenly the true nature of the meeting became clear to Rufus. His face reddened and his heart began to race. What could he possibly have done wrong? Had someone found out about the pen?

'But why?' he said, his heart pounding so hard he could feel the vibration in his ears.

'I'm afraid there's been an accusation of plagiarism,' said Mrs Stern, sitting back in her chair. 'They suspect you've copied someone else's work. It's a very serious allegation, Rufus, and one that could seriously embarrass the school.'

Rufus didn't know where to look, or what to

say. The principal was staring at him, arms folded, scrutinising his every twitch and tremble in the expectation that he would confess. It brought him to the brink of tears.

'But I didn't copy anyone's story,' he protested in a frightened voice. 'It really happened. I didn't copy anything. I swear I didn't.'

'I haven't said that you did, at least not knowingly. But sometimes these things happen. Sometimes something we've read, perhaps years ago, sticks in the back of our mind like a vague memory. Maybe that's what happened here?'

'It didn't. I didn't copy anything. I didn't. This isn't fair. I didn't do anything wrong.'

Rufus protested his innocence until he was breathless and crying, but Mrs Stern wasn't listening. She was too busy formulating theories. Roger Coyle had emailed her a copy of the 1996 story and she'd kept a copy of

Rufus's story on file. In her mind, the parallels were simply too many and too detailed. The only question to be resolved now, was how. If she could get to the bottom of that, she might find a way to lessen the embarrassment that was bound to fall upon the school, especially given all the publicity she'd gone out of her way to generate.

'Perhaps you went to the library and read something that you didn't realise you had remembered,' she went on, 'and some things slipped into your story without you realising? Perhaps you…'

Perhaps after perhaps, the accusations rained down on Rufus like fists. But as desperate as he was to prove his innocence, Mrs Stern was even more desperate for a confession. The least the boy could do, she thought, was come clean.

'For heaven's sake Rufus!' she protested shrilly. 'The Martello Tower? The old gentleman? The lessons in creative writing? I mean you didn't even have the wit to change the man's name!'

Rufus began to tremble.

Mrs Stern could see that he was becoming upset, but she was desperate to close the matter before Roger Coyle arrived the following day. She dreaded the prospect of an outsider coming into *her* school and telling her what was what.

'But I didn't,' pleaded Rufus with a cry of childish righteousness. 'I swear I didn't.'

'You go to the library, don't you?' Mrs Stern persisted.

'Yes, but…'

'And you'd often flick through books before deciding which of them to take out?'

'Sometimes, but I didn't take any…'

'I know, Rufus. But the book from which you are alleged to have copied is in the local library – I checked first thing this morning – or rather it *was* until recently. It appears to have gone missing. You must have read this book and forgotten about it, either that or…'

Rufus was distraught. His story would not be published. He would not get to see his name in print except, he now assumed, as a disgraced name in the newspapers. He didn't want Jonah to see that. It was cruel and unfair. But there was worse to come.

With an apologetic knock, Caroline Goode strolled into the room. She shot a disappointed look at Rufus and handed a small paperback to Mrs Stern.

'Class bookshelf,' she said solemnly. 'We must have missed it the first time. It appears to be from the municipal library.'

Rufus was shell-shocked. He didn't know where to look or what to say. Tears streamed down his face and his fists clenched in white-knuckled rage. Why wouldn't they believe him? He hadn't done anything wrong.

'That's not mine,' he cried desperately. 'I've never seen that book before.'

Mrs Stern pushed back her chair and drew herself up to her full height. 'I'm afraid the evidence speaks for itself,' she said with a judgemental tut and an angry glare. 'I hope you realise the seriousness of this. You've put us in a very difficult situation.'

'But I never... I didn't... The story's real.' Rufus's breath was becoming rapid and shallow; his clenched hands visibly shaking. 'It's not fair!' he bawled. 'I didn't. Someone must have...'

In desperation he looked to Miss Goode but, seeing her face closed against him, he panicked. Before either teacher could react he was out the door and running.

'RUFUS BLACK!' shouted Mrs Stern. 'COME BACK HERE THIS INSTANT!'

But Rufus wasn't listening. All he could hear were the accusations, roaring in his ears like a storm in a chimney.

'I hate this school,' he screamed as he pulled open the front door, 'and I hate everyone in it.'

As he reached the front gate his fury peaked. Without thinking, he picked up a rock from the flower beds and flung it angrily at Mrs Stern's car, which was sitting in the school driveway. It shattered the back windscreen.

'RUFUS!' Mrs Stern screamed from the porch. But it was too late. Rufus had gone.

Like a pair of startled ostriches, Mrs Stern and Miss Goode trotted as far as the gate but couldn't keep up in heels that were far too high for running. As Rufus disappeared, they shared a guilty look. They hadn't handled this well. Not well at all!

Rufus ran and ran and ran, as though the wind flowing through his blond locks could cool the anger that was burning inside his head. He ran and ran, carrying his wounded pride like an unsheathed sword, ready to lash out at anyone who tried to stop him. He ran till his heart was pounding on his ribs and his lungs were stretched to bursting.

He didn't see the car coming, but he heard the horn and the terrible screech of brakes. It didn't hit him, nor did he stop to see what happened to it, or indeed the driver. He just kept running, not daring to look back.

He'd reached the woods of the old psychiatric hospital before he finally allowed himself to stop. His head was spinning. He hadn't a clue what he was going to do next, not a single clue.

If the police hadn't been called to the school, he reasoned, they would surely have been called to the crash. At least he assumed the car had crashed. Either way, he was in BIG trouble. It would be all over the village in no time.

He was sorry now he hadn't listened to his

mother; sorry he'd ever met the old gentleman; sorry he'd allowed Monika to sway him; sorry he'd thrown that rock; sorry he hadn't looked before racing across that road. His mother would never forgive him. How could he possibly face her now? She would be so ashamed of him. So deeply ashamed.

Miss Goode was the last person Rufus would have expected to turn on him, and he would never forget the look of disappointment in her eyes. It hurt him, hurt him deeply.

After a short rest, he started to run again. But where was he to go? The police would surely call to his home. He hadn't thought, as he fled, about where he was going to sleep or what he was going to eat. Eaten alive by midges, and with no food or money, he could think of no one to turn to save for the mysterious old gentleman: a person he hadn't seen for months; a man who just minutes earlier he'd regretted ever having met; a man, he suddenly realised, he knew next to nothing about.

He wandered for hours, strolling aimlessly about the heavily wooded grounds of the hospital, waiting for it to get dark; certain that if he went to the Martello tower too early, he'd be seen and arrested. He had no idea if Persse would still be there, but it was all he could think of to do; the only place he could think of to go. Persse, he was convinced, would clear his name. Indeed, Persse O'Reilly was perhaps the only person who could.

'Susan, it's Judith Stern.'

Susan Black listened politely to Mrs Stern's explanations and self-justifications; her fingers clenched tightly about the phone. Too stunned to vent her fury, she left work immediately, pulling herself together just long enough to collect the twins.

Rufus still wasn't home by the time she

entered the apartment, but there was no need to panic, she thought. He would come home when he got hungry. He always did. But Rufus didn't come home that evening and, once the twins had been fed, she began to make some calls.

Alas, nobody knew where Rufus was. Some didn't even know *who* he was. Others were almost reproachful in tone; as if they thought it a bit rich that the parent of a child who had been allowed to roam at will should suddenly be fearful for his safety. One even suggested she try his *girlfriend's* house.

Had Rufus become interested in girls already? What else didn't she know? What else had she been too busy to notice?

A couple of mothers called back as soon as their husbands returned from work and offered to help search. A distressed and vulnerable child, after all, was a village emergency. These weren't people Susan knew, but she was too sick with worry to decline any offer of help.

She tried to wait by the phone, but she couldn't sit still. She felt helpless doing nothing. She wanted to be out there with them, doing *something*. But she couldn't leave the twins.

At length, she rang Lucy. She was starting to panic. She needed someone to mind the twins, she said, someone, anyone, to be close in case she got one of those 'is there someone who can come sit with you' visits.

'Oh, God!' exclaimed Lucy. 'I was afraid something like this might happen. I'll be right over.'

An hour later, Lucy turned up at the apartment to take the twins for a sleepover. If the worst happened, Susan did not want them to experience it first-hand. The twins weren't enthused, but a purposeful Susan pressed two packets of chocolate buttons into their hands and they left without the slightest suspicion of their mother's dread.

After they'd gone, Susan drove up and down the peninsula, battling to keep a lid on her panic. She searched all the places where Rufus might hide; calling and calling his name until, finally, she yielded to the inevitable and called the police.

Stories abounded in the locality about the Devil's Copse – a tiny, but densely planted, area of woodland within the grounds of the old psychiatric hospital. They told of ghosts, escaped madmen, and mysterious beings that howled all night. Parents cautioned children with colourful tales of boys and girls that had disappeared forever and many a campfire or Halloween bonfire had been enlivened with graphic and imaginative descriptions of what had been done to them.

No excuses were ever required, and no child

was ever taunted, for steering clear of the place. Occasionally it might arise as the subject of a dare, but the Devil's Copse was generally accepted as a place to be avoided. The fact that it lay within the grounds of an abandoned psychiatric hospital only strengthened the taboo. And yet, without the cover of the copse, it would be impossible for Rufus to reach the coast unseen, and he really wanted to get to Persse.

As darkness fell, the woods began to feel damp and musty, and Rufus to feel cold and vulnerable. Rising to his feet he began to thread his way beyond the walls of the old orchard and towards the edge of the copse. Skirting the fringes, he kept just enough inside the trees to remain unseen from the fields, but close enough to the edge to allow the moon to light his path.

His progress was slow. Maddeningly slow. He could barely see what was under his feet and had to pick his way through the tangled undergrowth with care. He'd barely covered a hundred metres when an unearthly sound sent a shiver down his spine.

'AAAAAA-AGHHH, AAAAAA-AGHHH.'

Rufus stood motionless, his heart thumping in his chest, his skin prickling. The sound came from deep within the copse. It sounded like a child in pain.

'AAAAA-AAGHHH, AAAAAA-AGHHH.'

Rufus shuddered involuntarily. The fields echoed with the cry and then, as it faded, with the sound of voices, advancing from the opposite direction. Torchlights were flickering behind the hedges of a distant field. A search party!

To stay where he was would mean certain discovery and arrest, but the only alternative to backing out into the open fields was to force his way through the mesh of low-hanging branches and head deeper into the copse... and *towards* the unearthly screams.

He moved cautiously, but branches and brambles tore at his arms and legs. More than once he had to bite his tongue to avoid crying out. The voices were gaining on him. When they got close enough for him to hear them clearly, he lay prostrate on the ground and, scarcely daring to breathe, waited for them to leave.

'You sure it came from here?' a man panted.

'Positive,' said another. 'Sounded like a child.'

Rufus recognised the second voice. It was Mr Thomas.

'Can't see a way in,' said the first man. 'Must be a track somewhere. Let's see if we can find a gap.'

Then it came again.

'AAAAAA-AGHHH, AAAAAA-AGHHH.'

The sound was louder this time, and a little less human.

'Chrissake!' exclaimed the first man. 'That's no child. It's a bloody vixen.'

'You sure?' said Mr Thomas doubtfully.

'Positive. You should hear them when they're mating. Proper racket! In the old days, folk used to think they were banshees. C'mon, we best get back and finish the golf course. There's no way the kid got through that thicket and no local kid is going in there. They say people have met the Devil in there. Serve the kid right if he did. Prison's a doddle these days. Took me the best part of an hour to clean up the mess outside the national school. Had to wash away the blood before the little ones arrive in the morning.'

Blood! Rufus' worst nightmare was confirmed. There could be no going back now. He waited for what seemed like hours but was probably no more than a few minutes. He waited until he was certain they had gone and then, scrambling to his feet, he brushed himself down and pushed deeper into the copse. Glancing back every few steps to make sure he wasn't being followed, he came upon a ditch that bordered a small clearing. An oak tree stood in the centre – a large oak with a trunk as wide as a car.

Obscured by one of the oak tree's giant roots, something moved. Rufus shifted his weight for a better look and a twig snapped beneath his foot. A curious head popped up from behind the root. It was the vixen. Rufus crouched down, as one might do to encourage a dog to come to you, but the vixen simply darted for the cover of the surrounding pines.

With the vixen gone, Rufus, climbed down into the ditch and attempted to climb out the other side. The ditch squelched as he stepped into it and his shoe came off in the mud. By the time he'd retrieved it and scaled the other side, his feet were caked in mud, the sleeve of his school sweater was torn and the bramble scratches on his arm were beginning to smart.

He looked back along the route he had come. If search parties were still out there, their torches no longer penetrated the woods. But he still could not relax. He did not want to be caught and sent to prison. He took a moment to survey his surroundings.

It was unusual, to say the least, to find an oak tree in the middle of a pine copse. Whoever had planted the pines must have lacked the heart to fell the oak. Circling it, he noticed slats nailed to the trunk, forming a wonky ladder that led through a trap door into some sort of treehouse.

The hut was a little smelly inside but, for the most part, it was dry. He felt his way along the walls until his hands came upon an old rug. He pulled it tightly around his shoulders to try to warm himself, but he couldn't relax. Every crackle in the undergrowth sounded like approaching footsteps; every rustling leaf a

whisper.

A treehouse doesn't just spring up in the middle of a wood. Someone has to build it; someone who would know that a child could hide inside. But it was dry and sheltered, and it was better than having to sleep outside.

The vixen screamed again from somewhere within the pines and set off the dogs in a distant housing estate. Rufus thought briefly of getting up to see if he could spot her, but he was too cold and too tired to shift himself and so he just sat there, staring out at the stars. Far from the lights of the village, they shone exceptionally bright in the night sky, sparkling like sequins on a black tapestry.

He tried to stay awake, but it was becoming slowly ever more difficult. His mind was exhausted. It wanted to rest. Several hours passed and his eyes slowly began to feel heavy and his body to jerk. In the end, he could withstand it no longer. He lay down on the wooden floor and before he knew it he had fallen asleep.

At 9.35 p.m. two uniformed Gardaí – a male sergeant and a young female officer – called to the apartment. They arrived in a squad car with flashing lights but no siren, sending the estate into a frenzy of twitching curtains. Until now, there had been a sense of unreality about Rufus's disappearance, but the sight of uniforms and the crackle of radios made it suddenly all too real.

The professional calm of the sergeant was temporarily infectious. He was a grey-haired man in his forties and, little by little, he managed to tease from Susan details of Rufus's age, height, and hair colour, and to record them in his notebook.

'Don't go worrying yourself unnecessarily,' he said. 'Most times they turn up safe and sound.' His soft Kerry accent inspired confidence, but 'most times' wasn't always.

The sergeant asked for a recent photo of Rufus, which Susan explained she didn't have, and then for a list of Rufus's friends, which she had also to confess she didn't know. Terrified that she was coming across as a negligent parent she rushed to justify her ignorance by explaining the family situation.

'We'll need a description of what he was wearing,' said the sergeant.

Susan went pale. 'Oh, God!' she cried desperately. 'What was he wearing? Why can't I remember?' The female garda took her by the arm and walked her to the bedroom and, through a process of elimination, they managed to complete a description. The female garda knew the drill; had been here before. But it was all taking so long!

All of a sudden, Susan found herself shivering; torn between the expectation of catastrophe and the hope that her son might at any minute walk sheepishly through that door, wondering what all the fuss was about. Her heart was fit to burst. The sergeant called his female colleague aside for a private word, then made his way to the door.

'We've enough to be getting on with,' he said as he left. 'Bríd will stay with you for the time being. Try not to use your phone, and while you're waiting, try to think of anything else that might be relevant.'

Waiting! He expected her to *wait*? To simply sit by the phone and speculate? How the hell was she supposed to do that when her son could be out there freezing to death?

'I'll put the kettle on,' said Bríd. 'You just sit down there and try to think of anywhere he might have gone, or anyone he might have gone to.'

Susan froze. She was staring at one of Rufus's copybooks. 'It's that man!' she cried suddenly. 'He's probably doing something

213

unspeakable to him as we speak. We need to go to the tower.'

'Calm down please Mrs Black,' said the female garda forcibly. 'What man is this?'

In an incoherent rush, Susan told her all about Persse O'Reilly. The garda asked for a description, but Susan could only refer her to the copybook that contained the story Rufus had written for the competition.

The garda scanned it briefly, then walked over to the window and rang her sergeant. The matter seemed suddenly to have become more urgent. In hushed tones, the words 'potential abduction' were finally spoken.

The sergeant went straight to the tower but found no one. He rang his colleague to tell her and then left to liaise with some of the parents that were searching the cliffs for Rufus. After that, it was a case of sitting and waiting, making endless mugs of tea, and reading through Rufus's stories with the female garda in search of further clues.

In the reading of those stories, Susan was struck by how many of Rufus's adult characters appeared to be clones of her husband – or at least of the husband she had known and loved before they had run out of things to say to each other.

'Oh, God!' she sighed sadly. 'Look at this. Magic! Invisibility! Super senses! The child is crying out for a sense of order and control. I've been such a fool. I thought I'd be enough for them. I thought in time they'd forget.'

The female garda took great care not to comment. She'd seen that look before, that crushing doubt, that sudden feeling of self-blame and self-loathing that always came hand-in-glove with cases of a missing child. She hated this part of the job. She didn't want to be there if a body was found, but she would be. She just knew that 'the lads' would leave it to her.

It was always the same. The parents always wanted to start over; to do things differently; to turn back time; always wondered how it could possibly have come to this. When the news was bad, her male colleagues always expected her to do the consoling. She hated that. It wasn't fair.

As night passed into morning, Susan found herself staring at Rufus's copybooks, trying hard to convince herself that no news was good news; wondering if her son was destined to become one of those missing children that never grew old: a photograph stuck in time, a poster on a lamppost, reprinted each year on the anniversary of his disappearance.

She wondered, too, if she would become one of those obsessive and hysterical mothers she'd seen so often on television: pathetic creatures with tear-streaked faces, appealing for information, doomed forever to see their missing child in the faces of other people's children. She stood up, intending to go to the bedroom to lie down for a bit.

'He's quite the talent, isn't he?' said Garda Bríd as she finished reading the last of the stories in Rufus's copybooks. 'You must be very proud of him.'

Susan was staring at Rufus's bed. It was exactly as he'd left it, unkempt and unmade. It reminded her of the morning she had checked herself out of the hospital and returned home to collect their passports. She had found the kitchen just as she'd left it, bloodstains and all. Nothing had changed, and yet everything had.

'Yes,' she said at length. 'Very proud.'

It was then, and only then, after so much panic and provocation, that Susan Black finally broke down and wept.

Rufus woke up shivering with cold. Weak daylight filtered through the door of the treehouse and overhead he could hear the cooing of a woodpigeon. It took him a moment to realise where he was. He looked down at his mud-caked jeans and boots and almost cried in despair. Blood! That was what the man had said. Someone was hurt or dead, and it was all his fault.

Carefully, he peeked out of the doorway. A crescent moon still hung in a washed-out dawn sky and the air was misty and damp. He listened hard for voices but heard none; wished he could go home, but daren't. He needed to find Persse. Persse would protect him. Persse would clear everything up. Persse would help him to find Jonah.

A bark shattered the silence. He edged himself to the door of the treehouse, half-expecting to see a police dog. But it was only the vixen. Once again she fled as soon as she saw him.

He'd had nothing to eat or drink for such a long time, and he really needed to pee. Looking carefully out of the door and window, to make sure there was no one about, he climbed down to the clearing and relieved himself behind a tree.

He hadn't slept well. In his dreams he had seen Mrs Stern and Miss Goode, telling him that he was a cheat. He also saw some strange woman he didn't know, calling him a murderer. Lastly, he saw a judge in a white wig telling him that he'd have plenty of time in prison to write stories and tell fibs. When finally he woke, he felt cold and exhausted.

Leaving the clearing he started to walk, trying to warm himself and searching for water to quench his thirst. It took longer than expected but, eventually, he found his way onto a track that led towards the coast. He stopped at a hedgerow to pick some blackberries, but even they couldn't take the edge of his thirst and his hand got cut on the thorns.

Tangled amongst the blackberries, he spotted some other fruit that was unfamiliar to him. Black and glossy, they looked a lot like overripe cherries. He tried one. It tasted sweet, so he had a couple more. Not knowing when he might eat again, he put a couple in his pocket for later.

It was still dark when Susan woke the following morning. A kettle was on the boil in the kitchen and the toilet was being flushed in the bathroom. She was lying on the sofa, covered by a duvet. The female garda must have thrown it over her at some stage during the night. She looked at the clock. 6.15 a.m. She had slept for less than three hours.

'Any word?' she asked in hushed tones as the garda came out of the bathroom.

'Nothing yet,' said Bríd, in a tone equally respectful of the hour.

She looked out the window. It was a clear

morning. A little misty but dry. She prayed Rufus was still alive, out there somewhere waiting to be found, and not locked in a dark basement somewhere. She thought briefly of Jonah, then pushed him from her mind.

'I'll be off soon,' said Bríd. 'My shift is over. Someone will be over shortly to talk to you. Is there anything I can do before I go? Someone to sit with you? A neighbour perhaps?'

'I don't know. To be honest, I don't know what I am supposed to do or what I'm supposed to be feeling. I can't think straight... I mean, what *should* I be doing?'

'Every case is different. All I can advise is that you look after yourself. Get some food delivered if you don't feel like cooking. Take it one step at a time. And you might want to ring work?'

'Oh, God! I'd have to talk to Dr Shah. He'll be full of questions. I don't think I can face that right now.'

'Leave it to me then. Here, get this down you. Two sugars wasn't it?'

When Roger Coyle was shown into the Fitzroy Room at 9.30 that morning, Judith Stern had just been on the phone to Susan Black and met with a torrent of abuse. She should have known the woman would have been watching the phone and that every ring would have been anticipated as the harbinger of disaster.

To make matters worse, here was this long-haired stranger walking smugly into her office to witness the guilty flush in her cheeks. Without standing to greet him, she beckoned him towards the empty seat in front of her desk.

'No sign?' asked Coyle, tidying his greying locks with a careless sweep of his hand.

'No,' she snapped. 'Nothing.'

'How much did you tell the boy?'

'Just that he'd been disqualified,' said Mrs

Stern dismissively, 'and the reason.'

'Did you tell him about me?'

'I hadn't time. We'd only just discovered the library book when he ran away. As for what he did to my car... well...'

'What library book?' Coyle cut across her.

'The one you mentioned over the phone. I have it here somewhere.'

Mrs Stern unearthed the book from under a pile of papers on her desk and passed it to Coyle. He opened the cover, stared at the lending record, then smiled knowingly.

'I think you have misjudged the boy.'

'And you would know this how?'

'Because, I think I know what has happened here, and if I'm right, then the boy is entirely innocent.'

'Would you care to elaborate?'

'Well, for a start, if you look at the lending record for this book, you will see that this book was on loan during the period that Rufus would have been writing his story and it has been loaned twice since.'

'That just goes to prove my point...'

'It would, if it had been Rufus who had borrowed it. But don't you think it strange that a person would borrow a book quite openly and then go back and steal it long after they'd returned it?'

'What exactly are you saying?'

'I'm saying that whoever stole this book, it most likely wasn't Rufus. I mean, even if he *had* copied from it, he would surely have finished with it long ago. If you check with the municipal library, I think you'll find that it wasn't Rufus who borrowed this book, and if it was on loan during the period he was writing, then he could hardly have copied from it.'

'And on the basis of that, you believe he is innocent?'

'There are other things; things I'd rather not discuss until I've spoken to him.'

'I suppose you're going to tell me now, that you know where to find him?'

'Possibly. Mrs Stern, let's just say that I've walked a few miles in this boy's shoes. Could you give me his mother's number or at least give her mine and ask her to ring me? And in the meantime, I'll hazard a guess that the book thief isn't sitting a million miles away from us right now. Someone who might have overheard you speaking on the matter perhaps?'

'Francie!' groaned Mrs Stern. 'Francie bloody McKellit!'

'Oh, God! Oh, God! Oh, God!' cried Susan, her lungs bursting with relief. Sitting with his back to the Martello Tower, his knees clutched to his chest, was her beloved firstborn, looking morose and forlorn, rocking gently back and forth as much for comfort as for warmth.

'Best you talk to him first,' said Roger Coyle as he turned off the engine. 'I'd have wagered we'd find him inside the tower, but no matter. He's safe.'

Rufus heard footsteps crunch on the pebbles behind him and lifted his head. His eyes met his mother's and she ran to him. Falling to her knees, she gathered his trembling body to her bosom, stroked his hair and kissed him in a frenzy of relief.

'I didn't cheat,' Rufus protested pitifully. 'Honest Mom, I didn't.'

'I know, Rufus,' cried Susan, taking off her coat and wrapping it tightly around him. 'She didn't mean it. She didn't understand. Where in God's name have you been? People have been out looking for you. They've been here several times. Where did you sleep?'

'I dunno. The woods. I caused a crash. Someone died.'

'It's okay Rufus. A secretary from the hospital came forward to say she'd spotted you. You gave her quite a fright, but she's fine. She hit a woodpigeon when she swerved to avoid you, but she's fine. No one died.'

Relief surged through Rufus's body.

'I got sick,' he said at length.

'I can see darling. I can see.'

Susan gave her son one last tight squeeze then helped him to his feet. There was a lot more she wanted to ask, but the last thing he needed right now was another interrogation. He was alive – a little smelly from the vomit – but otherwise unhurt. There would be plenty of time for questions later.

'Come on. Up you get,' she said. 'Let's get you home and out of those clothes. You must be frozen to the marrow. Oh, and there's someone I want you to meet.'

The first thing Susan did when she got back to the apartment was to get Rufus out of his soiled clothes and into the shower. She waited for Roger to leave, but he seemed reluctant, so she let him settle on her sofa. Her head still in a muddle, she went about clearing out the pockets of Rufus's soiled jeans.

'What have we got here then?' she said curiously. 'Cherries?'

Roger rose from his seat and came to take a look. 'My word!' he exclaimed. 'Your son has been remarkably fortunate.'

'What do you mean?'

'I mean these are Deadly Nightshade, sometimes called the Devil's Herb. They've been a mainstay of murder mysteries for centuries.'

'Poison? Should I be calling a doctor?'

'Their effect is frequently exaggerated, and he seems to be over the worst of it. It can be fatal in large doses, but it more commonly causes nausea and diarrhoea.'

When Rufus came out of the shower, dressed in his warmest pyjamas, Roger was waiting for him.

'How many of these have you eaten,' he asked.

'I dunno,' said Rufus. 'Two or three?'

'Lucky boy!' said Roger.

Susan couldn't decide which emotion to settle on. She had been bracing herself against grief, preparing herself for life without Rufus and her mind still couldn't let go of it, even in the face of such overwhelming relief. Desperate to conceal her emotions, she slipped away to the bedroom. Oblivious to her departure, Roger continued with his explanation.

'The plant was once believed to be the property of the Devil and if you ate the berries you would meet him face to face. Places where the plant grew wild would often refer to the Devil in their names, and stories would often be invented to keep children from going anywhere near it.'

'I thought they were cherries,' said Rufus

meekly.

'Well, you know better now. No harm done. Which brings me to your competition story. I've been waiting to tell you how much I, and the other judges, enjoyed it. You're a talented boy.'

Still suspicious of Roger, Rufus didn't respond to the flattery but seated himself on the far end of the sofa. When Susan finally returned, her eyes puffy and red, Rufus allowed her to wrap him in a warm duvet. It was only then that Roger noticed Susan's eyes. He felt suddenly awkward. He really should go, but he had unfinished business. They deserved an explanation, and he'd driven a long way to provide them with one.

'I was just saying,' he said, directing his remarks directly at Susan and raising his voice above the washing machine where Rufus's soiled clothes had started to spin, 'but for the issue of originality, Rufus might actually have won the competition.'

'But I didn't copy anything,' Rufus protested.

'I believe you, Rufus,' said Roger calmly. 'But the rules are very tight. It has to be an original story and, like it or not, the two stories are almost identical, even in the name of the old gentleman.'

'Mo-om?' Rufus whimpered anxiously.

'Please don't overreact, Rufus,' said Susan as she heated some tinned soup for him. 'Give the man a chance to explain.'

Rufus stared at his mother. She was speaking with an exaggerated calmness he didn't recognise. He'd never heard her use that tone of voice before.

'Tell me about the old gentleman,' said Roger. 'Describe him to me.'

Rufus described Persse, from his physical features to his manner of speech. He described the old-fashioned clothes; the dark circular glasses and wooden cane. As he rattled off each detail, Roger would nod.

'Tell me, Rufus,' said Roger when Rufus had finished. 'Do you think you could complete this verse for me?'

Clearing his throat and affecting a broad Dublin accent, Roger began to sing.

'Have you heard of one Humpty Dumpty, how he fell with a roll and a rumple, and curled up like Lord Olafa Crumple…'

The pronunciation was less marked and the rhythm slightly different, but it was the song that Persse was always singing to himself.

'By the butt of the Magazine Wall,' sang Rufus. 'Of the Magazine Wall. Hump, helmet and all.'

'Recognise it?' said Roger, enjoying Susan's bemusement.

'Should I?' said Susan.

'No reason why you should,' said Roger, 'unless you happened to be a Joycean scholar.

It's the ballad of Persse O'Reilly.'

'Persse wrote that?' Rufus broke in.

'I'm afraid not, Rufus,' said Roger. 'It was written by a certain James Joyce.'

'The man who invented Bloomsday!' trumpeted Rufus proudly.

'So, a writer and a scholar!' said Roger.

'Nah,' Rufus demurred. 'Persse told me. Did Joyce write a song about Persse?'

'No Rufus, he didn't. The man you know as Persse O'Reilly is actually a certain Benjamin Brewer – *Benny* to friends and family. It's a long story, and when your mother has finished making her calls to let everyone know you're safe, I'll tell you both about it.'

The story Roger told began with Benny Brewer's wife, giving birth to a little boy they christened James in honour of Benny's literary idol, the writer James Joyce.

'Inspired by the birth of his son,' said Roger, 'Benny set about writing a book in which he imagined an angry Joyce returning to Dublin as a ghost. The book was an instant success, but while Benny was on a publicity tour in the U.K. his wife and four-year-old son died following a gas leak at their home.'

'Poor man!' sighed Susan, moved to compassion by the recognition of the type of loss that only hours previous she had been expecting to be her own.

'Indeed!' said Roger. 'Benny blamed himself for not being there and six months after the funeral he walked out of his locksmith's shop, stuffed a mattress and blankets into the back of his van, and began a new life as an itinerant labourer, taking any work he could get his hands on.'

'There was a white van at the beach,' said Rufus.

'Could be his,' said Roger hurriedly. 'Then again, could be anyone's. Anyway, years later Benny was spotted chatting to a young boy outside the Martello Tower in Sandymount. By this time, he'd convinced himself that the deaths of his wife and son were the price that God had exacted from him for the loan of Joyce's talent.'

'He sounds dangerous to me!' remarked Susan.

'Trust me,' said Roger, 'Benny's harmless. But to get back to the story, armed with a pen and some coloured pencils, Benny would park himself each summer at a different Martello Tower and look for young boys with active imaginations to tutor in creative writing, as he had hoped one day to do with his own son. He called himself Persse O'Reilly after a character in one of Joyce's poems. The name is a corruption of *perce-oreille*, the French for earwig.'

'And that other story?' said Susan. 'The one from 1996? That was also about Brewer?'

'It was. I met him at the Sutton tower. I

never imagined when I wrote it that I'd get to read another.'

'It was you?' Rufus gasped.

'Yes, Rufus, and if it had been up to me there would not have been...'

'But how?' Rufus interrupted. 'How'd you learn all that other stuff? I mean he never spoke about himself. Not ever.'

'By accident, really. I was visiting my mother in St James' Hospital when I bumped into him visiting a woman in the same ward. He pretended not to know me, but after he'd left I popped over to have a chat with the woman. Turned out to be his sister, Maisie. It was her who told me his story. But enough about Benny, what about you, Rufus? Do you have any more stories? It's too late for the competition, of course, but I'd very much like to read them.'

Rufus was about to head to his bedroom to fetch his copybooks when he spotted them lying open on the coffee table. He looked to his mother. She nodded approvingly, then went to make some coffee.

Browsing through the first copybook, Roger was struck by how Rufus had taken the time to develop the personality and explore the motivation of *all* the main characters in his stories. This was not a common skill in writers of that age nor, indeed, was the obsession with fairness. Rufus's heroes were never entirely good, his villains never entirely bad. He wondered why that might be.

While Susan took a phone call from the twins, Roger's attention snagged on a story about baseball called *Quality Time*. It told of a child who gets lost in the crowd at a baseball game and somehow finds himself entering the players' dressing room.

'Baseball fan?' he asked.

'I guess,' said Rufus nervously.

Quality Time was based on memories of

sitting at games with his father's friends, laughing at jokes he didn't understand, and listening to language that he would never dare repeat. These fragmentary memories were precious to Rufus. He had never expected his mother to read them.

For years Rufus had scrupulously avoided doing anything that might upset the unspoken pact that allowed those baseball trips to continue. If Jonah had said to keep something a secret, then Rufus's lips were sealed tighter than the cap on a pillbox. 'What happens in Vegas, stays in Vegas,' they'd laugh together.

Not that his mother hadn't had her secrets too, but Rufus had always managed to find a separate place for those in his head. Not even by accident would he reveal one parent's secret to the other, most especially the hiding place in which his mother would squirrel away her rainy-day money.

Knowing that his mother had read his

stories made Rufus nervous. He was afraid she'd feel hurt again by his continued affection for his father. The last time was awful, he didn't want to back there.

'Wow!' said Roger at length. 'There is a lot in these. Do you mind if I hang on to them for a while?'

Rufus looked to his mother.

'Up to you,' she said.

'Will I get them back?' asked Rufus.

'You will of course,' said Roger. 'I'll leave my number and if you want them back at any stage your Mom can call me, OK?'

'I guess,' mumbled Rufus uncertainly.

'Right then,' said Roger, 'then I'll leave you to recover from your ordeals. I'll ring Mrs Stern tomorrow to concoct an excuse under which Rufus's story can be withdrawn without attracting any unwelcome attention. And don't worry about her windscreen. That's been taken care of.'

'You're very kind,' said Susan, 'but...'

'My pleasure,' said Roger firmly. 'If you have a paper and pen, I'll scribble down my contact details.'

Susan fumbled about in her handbag but couldn't find a pen, so she sent Rufus to fetch one. When Roger laid eyes on it, his jaw dropped.

'Where did you get this,' he asked solemnly.

'From Persse,' said Rufus. 'Why?'

'No reason,' he said. 'It's just very like one he gave to me once. You can't beat the scrape of a cold brassy nib. Isn't that right Rufus?'

Rufus nodded as Roger wrote out his number, smiling knowingly at the red ink that flowed from the nib.

'Right then, I must be off,' said Roger, draining his coffee. Looking directly at Susan he rolled his eyes towards the door.

'I'll walk you down,' she said.

They'd reached the lobby before Susan

spoke again. 'You know Rufus believes that pen does something to him when he uses it; makes him aware of his mistakes or something.'

'To tell you the truth, Mrs Black...'

Susan flinched. It felt suddenly odd to be called Mrs Black. She had always felt too young to be a 'Mrs' but the word grated now for other reasons.

'Susan,' she said, her face reddening.

'Well, Susan,' said Roger, 'it's like this. Editing your own stories can be tough, especially when you have to cut stuff you've worked hard on. By creating the myth of the pen, Benny allowed Rufus a taste of the most powerful spice in the universe.'

'Imagination?'

'Self-confidence. I was really attached to that pen myself. My teeth marks are still on it. Never did figure out where it had gone to. Look, I really must fly. I have a meeting at two.

It was nice meeting you. I'll be in touch.'

Somewhat self-consciously, Roger reached out to shake Susan's hand. Noting that he was not wearing a wedding ring, her own felt suddenly tight upon her finger.

As he drove away, Roger gave Susan a friendly wave, and she stood watching after him, waiting until he had turned the corner before turning back, lost in a girlish half-thought she hardly dared acknowledge. That night she removed her wedding ring, wrapped it in a tissue, and placed it at the back of her underwear drawer.

At the end of November, the results of the National Primary Schools Short Story Award were announced. No mention was made of Rufus Black's disqualification and no one seemed interested in why there were only eleven stories in the winners' anthology.

In the school newsletter, Mrs Stern

apologised on behalf of the school. The office, she said, had failed to notice that a parent's signature had been required on the application. As for Rufus, he hadn't thought that he would, but he enjoyed being back at school. Everyone was curious to know where he'd been hiding. But Rufus wasn't about to share knowledge of what he now considered to be *his* treehouse with anyone just yet.

Over the following weeks, he returned several times to the Martello tower. But he never saw Persse again. To Rufus, Benny Brewer would always be 'Persse'.

Rufus would remember that winter as a time of watching. Hardly an hour went past without his mother checking her phone for messages from Roger that she then would go to the bathroom to read. By Halloween Roger's visits had become regular. They had begun with the return of Rufus's copybooks, then quickly progressed to the sharing of books. In no time at all Roger no longer needed an excuse.

As the twins began to anticipate Santa they also attempted to teach Roger some of the irreverent festive songs that Jonah had once delighted in teaching them. Susan found herself watching and listening with a mounting sense of alarm. And then, one day, it finally happened.

'Mom?' said Annika. 'How will Santa know where to find us? How will he know we're not living in Normal anymore?'

'Santa has ways of keeping track of good children,' said Susan softly, attempting to reassure them but no longer able to conceal the strain. 'No one knows how he does it, but he always manages to find them.'

'What about Dad?' said Chlöe finally. 'Will he know where to find us?'

Susan cast a pained look at Roger, then turned away. Rufus could see she was afraid, not of Jonah coming back, but of Roger's reaction to the twins' unthinking chatter.

'Your dad knows how to get in touch,' Roger quickly intervened, 'and I'm sure he will, some day, when he feels ready. But whatever about your dad writing, isn't there another letter that's perhaps even more urgent?'

The twins exchanged a puzzled look.

'You haven't finished your Santa letters yet and tomorrow is the last day for posting. Santa may well be able to find you, but he's not a mind reader. If you don't tell him what you want, he'll have to guess.'

Annika looked at Chlöe, and they both looked at Susan, whose silent nod sent the twins racing to begin their letters.

'Thank you,' Susan mouthed emotionally as she went to help the twins.

A new routine had evolved whereby, in order to 'give Susan a break' Roger would bring the children to play centres, cinemas, and swimming pools at weekends. Only Susan didn't always want a break and often came too. Roger also insisted on driving Rufus to away matches with his soccer team.

Without ever once staying the night – for there was nowhere for him to sleep, Roger settled into the routine of their fractured family life. He and Susan would often sit up late talking, and Rufus often fell asleep to the muffled hum of their voices.

The children quickly grew fond of Roger *and* to depend on him. If Roger promised to do something, he did. If you wanted to talk, he listened. Little by little, he began to fill the space that Jonah had once filled, and the children began to feel part of a regular family again.

But it wasn't only the children's lives that were brightening: Susan, too, seemed to have discovered a new mood or to have rediscovered an old one. She even began to sing again, something the children hadn't heard her do since they left Normal. And it wasn't only her *mood* that was changing!

The children had never known their mother as a woman who took pains with her appearance, or who became excitedly indecisive in front of an open wardrobe. But, all of a sudden, she started to look younger, more girlish, and prettier. It was, as Chlöe remarked one day, like having a new mom. She even found the strength to make a long-distance phone call to Normal to drop the charges against Jonah.

On Christmas morning Roger arrived with books for everyone and stayed for the entire day, as indeed did Lucy, carrying a couple of family albums from their childhood. Susan didn't even protest when Lucy gifted Rufus a mobile phone – something Susan had always been opposed to in the past.

'Well, at least he'll be able to ring someone

if he gets into bother,' she conceded.

Occasionally, in their excitement, one of the children would remember an incident or a family tradition from their old life, but Roger never seemed to mind. That was *their* past, he understood, not his. *His* time was only beginning.

Roger had by now become such a presence in their lives that, one day, Rufus realised he could no longer remember the sound of Jonah's voice. It shocked him how quickly such things could be forgotten. They hadn't even got a photograph of Jonah to remember him by.

He wondered, too, if Jonah was forgetting *them*. And he wasn't the only one. One night, as he was reading the twins a bedtime story, Chlöe looked long and hard into his eyes.

'Rufus,' she said, 'will we have to call Roger *Daddy* if we go to live with him?'

'Who said anything about living with him?'

'Nobody, I just thought.'

'Well don't. You'll jinx it. But I'm pretty sure Roger won't want to be called anything but Roger.'

'That's okay then,' said Chlöe. 'I don't want two dads. Can we have the starfish story again?'

Rufus had never mentioned the matter of surnames to anyone, but he *had* thought about it. Their surname was a link in a chain: a chain that tied them to Jonah, and to Jonah's family. It was half of who they were. Could they really be made to break it? And would Jonah ever be able to find them if they did? With every passing day, it seemed that Jonah Black was drifting further and further away from them.

'Rufus, come here a minute honey,' cried Susan suddenly. 'Roger has something to tell you.'

His mother sounded excited and instantly Rufus found himself hoping it would be about a house: a house in which they would all live together; a house in which he'd get his own room, where he could dream of who and what he wanted without fear of betraying himself to his mother.

'Come and sit here, Rufus,' said Roger, smiling broadly.

Rufus looked to his mother, half-expecting her to want to break the news herself, like the day she told him about the imminent arrival of the twins. But Susan simply motioned him to pay attention. The news was Roger's then. Not hers. Not theirs.

'A while ago,' said Roger, 'I showed your stories to a friend who's really into the idea of books *by* kids *for* kids. Your stories will need editing, of course, but she would like to publish them. All you have to do is sign this contract here. Your mum has already signed.'

Rufus could scarcely contain himself. 'Mom?' he gasped excitedly. 'Is it true?'

'Every word,' said Susan, flinging her arms

around him. 'We had to wait until after the competition results were announced to tell you. Questions might have been asked, and that wouldn't have been fair on the winner. But isn't it just the best?'

'Deadly!' cried Rufus, as the twins looked on admiringly. Everything felt suddenly different. Things were going to be okay. He just knew they were.

'The Singing Stones' was officially launched at a city centre hotel the following May. There were about fifty guests present on the night, including Judith Stern and Caroline Goode. Neither had been entirely forgiven by Rufus, but he had only four weeks left in primary school and he figured he could manage to be gracious until then.

His mother was also there, holding hands with Roger, moving easily amongst the gathering and accepting countless fleeting compliments on her son's behalf. Rufus felt mildly embarrassed at this because none of the other parents were holding hands.

Nipper came in a grey suit, a red dickie-bow, and his signature flat cap. The cap raised the occasional eyebrow, but it was Monika's arrival that really caught everyone's attention. In her three-quarter length concert dress and two-inch heels, she could easily have passed for sixteen. Her mother was just as glamorous. They looked like movie stars.

'Congratulations,' said Monika, bending slightly to give Rufus a very public hug and holding it so long that his face burned hotter than the day he ate the deadly nightshade. He didn't like that she was taller than him in heels. He felt like a clumsy child beside her; prayed she wouldn't try to kiss him and leave lipstick on his cheek.

'I suppose this means you're going to be famous,' Nipper broke in with a backhanded compliment.

'I don't know,' said Rufus, self-consciously disentangling himself. 'Maybe a little.'

'A little!' exclaimed Monika dramatically. 'God, you must be the coolest kid in school right now.'

'You think?' said Nipper, pulling his hands together. '*Coolest* kid in school?'

'DON'T!' pleaded Monika.

'Don't what?' said Nipper, cracking his knuckles.

'Too late!' groaned Monika and Rufus in unison.

'By the way,' Rufus suddenly blurted. 'I've found a clubhouse. Just for us. In the woods.'

'Oh Rufus,' gushed Monika with a wicked glint. 'That's so romantic. I didn't think you had it in you!'

Rufus blushed, again. 'For all of us,' he parried hastily; cringing inwardly at his own cowardice.

'Oh!' sighed Monika theatrically. 'Go on then, tell us. Where is it?'

'An abandoned treehouse. Hasn't been used for years.'

'Where?' Nipper broke in. 'Was that where you were hiding?'

Rufus tapped his nose. 'All in good time,' he said. 'Can't talk about it here. My mom doesn't even know. It will be our secret.'

There was a formal speech that night from the book's editor, Sally Jackson of Mansell & Mansell. 'I think we can all agree that this book represents an extraordinary achievement for a thirteen-year-old,' she said, 'and that he has brought distinction to his school, his village, and his family. I think it's time we showed him how proud we are of him.'

There followed a thunderous round of applause and several loud cheers that made Rufus tremble. He looked up at his mother.

Tears were streaming down her cheeks.

'I'm so proud of you darling,' she said softly. 'And I know Jonah would be too.'

A lump formed in Rufus's throat. He knew how much it had cost his mother to say that. It took a deep stuttering breath to stop him from breaking down in tears.

When the applause died down Sally Jackson called on Rufus to say a few words. Rufus looked to Susan. Nobody had warned him about this. As he turned to face the room, he became paralysed by fear, so Susan said a few words on his behalf. She concluded with the announcement that Roger had a surprise for him.

'A little present,' said Roger handing Rufus a brown paper parcel, 'to mark the occasion.'

'Whoa there, tiger!' Susan laughed, as her son tore excitedly at the wrapping.

Rufus's jaw dropped. It was an old book – *Finnegan, Begin Again* by Benjamin Brewer –

and it was signed by the author on the inside flap. In red ink!

Rufus could contain the tears no longer. They dribbled down his cheek and sent the assembly into rapturous applause. Overcome by the general goodwill, Rufus gave Roger the biggest hug he'd ever given any man, Jonah included.

On the way home from school the following day, after he'd parted company with Monika and Nipper, Rufus called into the post office. For the first time since he'd left Normal, he'd felt the urge to write to his old friends back home. He'd been too embarrassed before, but he had something worth telling now.

Secretly he was hoping that they would write back, and tell him without having to be asked, what had become of their old house, and of Jonah.

After he'd posted the letters, he purchased a

jiffy bag into which he slipped one of the six free copies of his book he'd been given by the publisher. He wrote nothing inside the book and did not include a letter.

'Gideon Black,' the postmistress remarked as she weighed the parcel. 'Unusual name. Are you sure you've got that right?'

'My grandfather,' explained Rufus.

Sales of Rufus's book proved steady but unspectacular. Nevertheless, some fan mail began to dribble into the publisher's office. The first batch was delivered to the apartment that August while Rufus was out swimming with Monika at Tower Bay. Just he and Monika. No Nipper. He was late home because Monika had wanted to explore the smugglers' caves, hoping to find some relics of times past uncovered at low tide.

'A package arrived for you while you were out,' said his mother as he burst brightly into the apartment, 'from the publisher.'

'Where is it?'

'I left it on your bed.'

Rufus ran to his bunk, tore open the envelope, and emptied the letters onto the duvet. Amongst the many little white and blue envelopes, his eyes lit upon a postcard with an American stamp.

'Your stories are awesome!' was all that was written on the card. No address, and no signature. Just a phone number: a very long phone number. The handwriting looked familiar and the postmark said San Diego, California. He didn't know anyone in San Diego and didn't recognise the number. He turned over the card. On the front was a photograph of a breaching whale!

His heart skipped a beat. He looked over his shoulder to make sure his mother wasn't watching, then took out his phone and sent a simple text.

'Dad?'

At that moment a train flew past, sounding its horn as it raced through Donabate station. On this occasion, the sound did not bring to mind a night of spilt blood and flashing lights. Rather, it brought to mind a movie about three children, a railway, and an absent father who was eventually returned to his family.

MARTELLO TOWERS

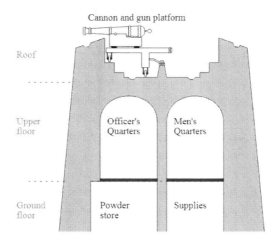

Martello Tower Layout - Public Domain via Wikimedia Commons.

IN 1804, AFRAID that Napoleon might try to invade Ireland, the British built about fifty Martello Towers along Ireland's coast. Twenty-six were built in and around Dublin Bay.

The towers were two storeys high with a flat roof on which a cannon was placed. The walls were built 2.4m thick to withstand enemy cannon fire. They were usually two stories high and could house a garrison of 15-20 soldiers.

The towers were built in sight of each other so that they could communicate with each other and warn of French naval attacks. The one in Donabate is known as No. 6 Tower.

The most famous Martello tower in Ireland is the tower Sandycove, Dublin, where James Joyce spent six nights in 1904. The opening scenes of his 1922 novel *Ulysses* take place here. The tower has become a place of pilgrimage for Joyce enthusiasts, especially on 'Bloomsday', which takes place on June 16th.

THE EVANS
MEMORIAL TOWER

The Evans Memorial Tower © Gerard Ronan 2021

THE ROUND TOWER in Portrane was built, about 1843, by Sophia Evans of Mount Evans, in memory of her late husband, the member of parliament for Dublin, George Evans. It was the first round tower to have been built on Irish soil since the Norman invasion and it started a trend of memorial round towers. A bust of George Evans used to sit in the doorway of the tower, but this was removed by a family member in the 1930s or 1940s.

Sophia Evans was an extraordinary woman for her day. She met two Queens, the divorced wife of a King, and possibly even the Emperor and Empress of France. Largely self-educated, she was close to both the Darwin and Condorcet families and was a daughter and sister to three of the most famous Irish politicians of her day. Sophia also helped, with the aid of her steward, William Kelly, to greatly mitigate the effects of the Great Famine in her locality.

George Evans died in 1842, and his wife, Sophia, in 1853. They were buried in the ruins of Saint Catherine's Church in Portrane. They are best remembered locally for establishing the primary schools which later became St. Patrick's Boys' National School and Scoil Phádraic Cailíní.

JAMES JOYCE

James Joyce. Illustration by Derry Dillon

BORN IN DUBLIN, in February 1882, James Joyce was the second of 10 children. Considered one of the most significant writers of the 20th century, he began a new style of writing called 'stream of consciousness'. This style allows a character's thoughts, feelings, and reactions all to be written in an uninterrupted flow.

Joyce's experimental work caused a

sensation at the time and he has influenced many other writers. His most famous book is *Ulysses* (1922), which follows the wanderings through Dublin of a man called Leopold Bloom over the course of a single day. Bloom's encounters mirror those of Ulysses in Homer's epic Greek poem, *The Odyssey*.

Joyce's *Ulysses* was considered very controversial in its day. It was seen as an attack on both governments and Church and was banned in the USA and the UK. Persse O'Reilly's mannerisms in this novel are heavily influenced by Joyce's language in *Finnegan's Wake*.

All of Joyce's books are set in Ireland, but he lived most of his life in France and Switzerland. He died on January 13, 1941, in Zürich, Switzerland, and is buried alongside his wife in Fluntern Cemetery. His life is celebrated annually in Ireland on June 16, with a literary festival known as Bloomsday.

ACKNOWLEDGEMENTS

I owe particular thanks to Zoe Stephenson and Ellen Gavigan for their editorial assistance and advice, to Derry Dillon for his wonderful illustrations and Marcel Koortzen for proofreading the completed novel.

Special thanks are also due to Helen O'Donnell, Betty Boardman, and the staff of the County Archives in Fingal County Council, for their continued support over several years now, of my efforts to document many of the lives and legends of the Portrane Peninsula. Finally, I owe the usual debt of gratitude to my wife, Cliona, and my daughter, Eleanor, for their continued forbearance and support.

TALES OF OLD TURVEY

OTHER BOOKS
IN THE SAME SERIES

The Legend of Gobán

GERARD RONAN

Illustrated by Derry Dillon

Born in the Kingdom of Turvey, near Donabate, in north County Dublin, Gobán Saor was the greatest craftsman and builder in Ireland. But he was also, reputedly, one of the smartest Irishmen who ever lived. Long after his buildings had been forgotten, people still told fireside stories of his gripping adventures and the clever ways he outsmarted his enemies.

The Legend of Joseph Daw

GERARD RONAN

Illustrated by Derry Dillon

Rescued from a shipwreck at the age of four, Joseph Daw is taken as an unpaid servant by a family of smugglers from Turvey, a townland in north County Dublin close to the village of Donabate. Despite a life of hardship and cruelty, he grows up to be a quiet and honest youth, very different from his masters. But, just as he finds the courage to escape, he chances to witness an event that changes everything, and not for the better.

Lucky Kate

GERARD RONAN

Illustrated by Derry Dillon

Orphaned and homeless at the age of sixteen, Kate Ryan is sent to the county workhouse at Balrothery where, after three years of picking oakum, she is offered the opportunity of a lifetime.

To save on the cost of caring for them, the workhouse guardians are offering to pay the passage of three young women to the new colonies in Australia, where there is a shortage of women. Tickets have already been booked for them on the largest passenger ship ever built – the *Tayleur*. It is a voyage that will change Kate's life forever.